S0-BAJ-321

OPPOSING VIEWPOINTS® SERIES

The US Military

WITHDRAWN

Other Books of Related Interest

Opposing Viewpoints Series

America's Changing Demographics
Feminism
Gender in the 21st Century
Interpreting the Bill of Rights
Toxic Masculinity

At Issue Series

Civil Disobedience
Cyberwarfare
The Federal Budget and Government Spending
Gender Politics
The Opioid Crisis

Current Controversies Series

America's Mental Health Crisis
Are There Two Americas?
Drones, Surveillance, and Targeted Killings
Enhanced Interrogation and Torture
Returning Soldiers and PTSD

"Congress shall make no law … abridging the freedom of speech, or of the press."

First Amendment to the US Constitution

The basic foundation of our democracy is the First Amendment guarantee of freedom of expression. The Opposing Viewpoints series is dedicated to the concept of this basic freedom and the idea that it is more important to practice it than to enshrine it.

OPPOSING
VIEWPOINTS®
SERIES

| The US Military

Avery Elizabeth Hurt, Book Editor

GREENHAVEN
PUBLISHING

Published in 2022 by Greenhaven Publishing, LLC
353 3rd Avenue, Suite 255, New York, NY 10010

Copyright © 2022 by Greenhaven Publishing, LLC

First Edition

All rights reserved. No part of this book may be reproduced in any form
without permission in writing from the publisher, except by a reviewer.

Articles in Greenhaven Publishing anthologies are often edited for length to meet page
requirements. In addition, original titles of these works are changed to clearly present
the main thesis and to explicitly indicate the author's opinion. Every effort is made to
ensure that Greenhaven Publishing accurately reflects the original intent of the authors.
Every effort has been made to trace the owners of the copyrighted material.

Cover image: Bumble Dee/Shutterstock.com

Library of Congress Cataloging-in-Publication Data

Names: Hurt, Avery Elizabeth, editor.
Title: The United States military / Avery Elizabeth Hurt.
Description: First edition. | New York : Greenhaven Publishing, 2022. |
  Series: Opposing viewpoints | Includes bibliographical references and
  index. | Contents: The US military | Audience: Ages 15+ | Audience:
  Grades 10–12 | Summary: "Anthology of diverse perspectives that
explore many issues pertaining to the US military, with resource
material and introductory material."— Provided by publisher.
Identifiers: LCCN 2020049266 | ISBN 9781534507562 (library binding) | ISBN
  9781534507548 (paperback)
Subjects: LCSH: United States—Armed Forces. | United States—Military
  policy.
Classification: LCC UA23 .U546 2022 | DDC 355.00973—dc23
LC record available at https://lccn.loc.gov/2020049266

Manufactured in the United States of America

Website: http://greenhavenpublishing.com

55.00973

1S

Contents

Chapter 3: Who Should Be Allowed to Serve?

Chapter 4: Does the US Do Enough for Its Veterans?

The Importance of Opposing Viewpoints

Perhaps every generation experiences a period in time in which the populace seems especially polarized, starkly divided on the important issues of the day and gravitating toward the far ends of the political spectrum and away from a consensus-facilitating middle ground. The world that today's students are growing up in and that they will soon enter into as active and engaged citizens is deeply fragmented in just this way. Issues relating to terrorism, immigration, women's rights, minority rights, race relations, health care, taxation, wealth and poverty, the environment, policing, military intervention, the proper role of government—in some ways, perennial issues that are freshly and uniquely urgent and vital with each new generation—are currently roiling the world.

If we are to foster a knowledgeable, responsible, active, and engaged citizenry among today's youth, we must provide them with the intellectual, interpretive, and critical-thinking tools and experience necessary to make sense of the world around them and of the all-important debates and arguments that inform it. After all, the outcome of these debates will in large measure determine the future course, prospects, and outcomes of the world and its peoples, particularly its youth. If they are to become successful members of society and productive and informed citizens, students need to learn how to evaluate the strengths and weaknesses of someone else's arguments, how to sift fact from opinion and fallacy, and how to test the relative merits and validity of their own opinions against the known facts and the best possible available information. The landmark series Opposing Viewpoints has been providing students with just such critical-thinking skills and exposure to the debates surrounding society's most urgent contemporary issues for many years, and it continues to serve this essential role with undiminished commitment, care, and rigor.

The key to the series's success in achieving its goal of sharpening students' critical-thinking and analytic skills resides in its title—

Opposing Viewpoints. In every intriguing, compelling, and engaging volume of this series, readers are presented with the widest possible spectrum of distinct viewpoints, expert opinions, and informed argumentation and commentary, supplied by some of today's leading academics, thinkers, analysts, politicians, policy makers, economists, activists, change agents, and advocates. Every opinion and argument anthologized here is presented objectively and accorded respect. There is no editorializing in any introductory text or in the arrangement and order of the pieces. No piece is included as a "straw man," an easy ideological target for cheap point-scoring. As wide and inclusive a range of viewpoints as possible is offered, with no privileging of one particular political ideology or cultural perspective over another. It is left to each individual reader to evaluate the relative merits of each argument— as he or she sees it, and with the use of ever-growing critical-thinking skills—and grapple with his or her own assumptions, beliefs, and perspectives to determine how convincing or successful any given argument is and how the reader's own stance on the issue may be modified or altered in response to it.

This process is facilitated and supported by volume, chapter, and selection introductions that provide readers with the essential context they need to begin engaging with the spotlighted issues, with the debates surrounding them, and with their own perhaps shifting or nascent opinions on them. In addition, guided reading and discussion questions encourage readers to determine the authors' point of view and purpose, interrogate and analyze the various arguments and their rhetoric and structure, evaluate the arguments' strengths and weaknesses, test their claims against available facts and evidence, judge the validity of the reasoning, and bring into clearer, sharper focus the reader's own beliefs and conclusions and how they may differ from or align with those in the collection or those of their classmates.

Research has shown that reading comprehension skills improve dramatically when students are provided with compelling, intriguing, and relevant "discussable" texts. The subject matter of these collections could not be more compelling, intriguing, or urgently relevant to today's students and the world they are poised to inherit. The anthologized articles and the reading and discussion questions that are included with them also provide the basis for stimulating, lively, and passionate classroom debates. Students who are compelled to anticipate objections to their own argument and identify the flaws in those of an opponent read more carefully, think more critically, and steep themselves in relevant context, facts, and information more thoroughly. In short, using discussable text of the kind provided by every single volume in the Opposing Viewpoints series encourages close reading, facilitates reading comprehension, fosters research, strengthens critical thinking, and greatly enlivens and energizes classroom discussion and participation. The entire learning process is deepened, extended, and strengthened.

For all of these reasons, Opposing Viewpoints continues to be exactly the right resource at exactly the right time—when we most need to provide readers with the critical-thinking tools and skills that will not only serve them well in school but also in their careers and their daily lives as decision-making family members, community members, and citizens. This series encourages respectful engagement with and analysis of opposing viewpoints and fosters a resulting increase in the strength and rigor of one's own opinions and stances. As such, it helps make readers "future ready," and that readiness will pay rich dividends for the readers themselves, for the citizenry, for our society, and for the world at large.

Introduction

> *"It is a proud privilege to be a soldier—a good soldier [with] discipline, self-respect, pride in his unit and his country, a high sense of duty and obligation to comrades and to his superiors, and a self-confidence born of demonstrated ability."*
>
> —*General George S. Patton*

One beautiful October day in 1967, at the height of the Vietnam War, anti-war demonstrators decided that the Pentagon, the headquarters of the United States Department of Defense, needed not just a protest, but an exorcism. They planned to accomplish this by using a mystical ritual to cause the building to levitate 300 feet above the ground, turn orange, and vibrate until all the evil energies were shaken out of it.

Some thirty-five thousand people gathered for the event. They sang, chanted, and hugged each other to promote loving vibrations. Some waved American flags; some attempted to burn flags. As far as anyone could tell, the building stayed firmly anchored to its foundation. And for evil energies … well, who knows? But a few years later—after a great many more protests—the United States signed a peace treaty with North Vietnam. The poet Allen Ginsberg, one of the organizers of the Pentagon event, claimed success, saying the demonstration "demystified the authority of the military."

The US military's authority survived, more or less intact, despite Ginsberg's claims and the end of America's involvement in the Vietnam War. Levitating the Pentagon was more of a publicity stunt than anything else, designed to draw attention to the anti-war cause. However, this singular incident, strange and quixotic as it was, may be the perfect symbol of the often-troubled relationship between the people of the United States and the nation's military. During popular wars, Americans support their military proudly. During unpopular wars or wars that have outlasted their welcome, Americans question the values and policies that lead to a huge military, seemingly unending wars, and the deaths of tens of thousands of innocents, both American and foreign.

One of the primary roles of a government is to protect its people, whether from enemies microbial or human. When it comes to protecting them from human enemies, that usually requires a military. In the United States, that military is accountable to the citizenry as well as to the government. Civilian control of the military is embedded in the US Constitution. The president, an elected official, is the commander in chief of the armed forces. The US secretary of defense must be chosen from civilians rather than active or recently retired military. Congress, an elected body, is in charge of allocating funds for the military as well as declaring war. The Founders intended the public to be ultimately in charge of the composition and scope of the US military. Americans have taken that responsibility to heart, though rarely agreeing on the details.

In *Opposing Viewpoints: The US Military*, viewpoint authors look at the many complex issues surrounding the United States military and the relationship between that military and the taxpayers who fund it in chapters titled "Should There Be a Universal Service Requirement in the United States?" "Should the US Increase or Decrease Military Spending?" "Who Should Be Allowed to Serve?" and "Does the US Do Enough for Its Veterans?"

In chapter 1, the viewpoints take on the question of how the United States should staff its military. Which is best: an all-volunteer army or a draft?

The authors represented in chapter 2 turn to the question of the military budget. Does the United States spend too much or too little on defense? Can the nation justify a huge military budget when so many of its children live in poverty, with food insecurity a daily experience and health care a privilege that only some can afford? Or do the particular threats of today's world—terrorism, both foreign and domestic—call for even higher levels of defense spending?

Americans also vigorously debate the question of who should be allowed to serve in the military. In chapter 3, the authors examine the debate over whether women should be allowed to serve in combat positions and whether LGBTQ Americans should be allowed to serve at all.

Despite Americans' mixed feelings about the military, the public virtually always supports the men and women—their fellow citizens—who serve in these conflicts. Or they intend to. Still, servicepeople often have difficulty adjusting to civilian life, and questions have arisen about the physical and mental toll war takes on our soldiers. Chapter 4 asks the question, "Do we do enough for our veterans?"

When it comes to demonstrating their patriotism, some Americans display flags and sing the national anthem. Others display signs and sing protest songs. Some even try to levitate the Pentagon. But no matter how varied their opinions are, one thing made clear in this volume is that Americans care deeply about their military and the men and women who serve. They just have a lot of different opinions about how that military should be staffed, how it should be paid for, and what it should ultimately do.

CHAPTER 1

Should There Be a Universal Service Requirement in the United States?

Chapter Preface

Compulsory military service, also known as conscription or simply the draft, has been a contentious point in the United States for as long as the nation has existed. The draft was used to recruit military personnel in the American Revolution, the Civil War, both World Wars, the Korean War, and most recently (and famously), the Vietnam War.

The active draft ended in 1973 amidst widespread anti-war and anti-draft protests. However, the Selective Service—the government system for managing a draft—still operates. In 1980, President Jimmy Carter reinstated the requirement for registration. Today, all males between 18 and 25 years of age must register so that they can be called up in case there is a need to quickly boost the size of the military.

Even without an active draft, the United States has managed to prosecute decades of war in Afghanistan and Iraq, as well as military operations in many other places, without resorting to conscription.

The viewpoints in this chapter take a variety of positions on the benefits and necessity of drafting citizens to serve in the military. Some argue that an all-volunteer military has been proven more efficient and effective than a military made up of conscripts. Others point out that people who are forced to serve rarely make good service members. In addition, it isn't cost-effective to train and provide benefits for people who are not likely to reenlist after their required term of service is over. On the other hand, some authors make the case that compulsory military service is necessary to be prepared for unexpected wars. Aside from those concerns, some viewpoints argue that an all-volunteer military leads to a dangerous disconnect between the citizenry and the military. One viewpoint equates the draft with slavery. The last viewpoint makes a case for compulsory national service but does not limit that service to the military.

| "I would rather have a hundred courageous volunteers . . . than a thousand reluctant warriors."

America Does Not Need a Draft

Kevin Ryan

In the following viewpoint, Kevin Ryan examines the idea that an all-volunteer military is not practically or socially beneficial. The author rebuts several of the most common arguments for reinstating a peacetime draft, including the oft-made claim that military members come primarily from the poor and uneducated classes. He finds all of these arguments wanting. Brigadier General (retired) Kevin Ryan is an associate fellow at Harvard Kennedy School's Belfer Center for Science and International Affairs and former US defense attaché to Russia.

As you read, consider the following questions:

1. What is meant by a "peacetime draft," as described in this viewpoint?
2. What, according to the author, was the original reason for supporting an all-volunteer military force in the US?
3. What role did the Reserves and National Guard play in shifting to an all-volunteer force?

"America Does Not Need a Draft," by Kevin Ryan, Center for the National Interest, August 30, 2018. Reprinted by permission.

Nick De Gregorio, a veteran of our nation's current wars, recently wrote an article for the *National Interest* in which he argued for the return to a military draft as a way to not only help the military but also to involve our nation's citizens in service to their country. He is not alone in this thinking. Many outstanding citizens of our country argue for a draft. General (retired) Stanley McChrystal, my classmate from West Point, is one proponent.

But this sincere interest in helping our military and instilling a sense of service to our country by reinstating the draft is wrongheaded. We don't need a draft to "spread the pain" (or privilege) of military service among various social and economic groups, and it would end up costing the military way more in money, means and morale than we can afford. Using De Gregorio's earnest piece, which lays out the most common arguments for a draft, we can examine whether those arguments hold up to scrutiny.

Up front it is important to note that our nation still requires young men to register for "selective service" (draft), and Congress, with the president, can reinstate a draft if a conflict were so big as to require a major increase in the military. What De Gregorio and others are recommending though is a "peace time" draft.

It is also important to recognize that both De Gregorio and I agree that our current volunteer force has, in his words, "enabled America to sustain its military pre-eminence." In that regard, the All Volunteer Force (AVF) meets our national interests. Where De Gregorio and I differ is in assessing how an all-volunteer force affects our national character and our national will. De Gregorio thinks the AVF undermines those things. I do not.

> Through the 1973 War Powers Resolution (WPR), the United States committed to never again enable the president to prosecute lengthy wars without the express consent of Congress.

De Gregorio claimed in his article that the All Volunteer Force was initiated along with the 1973 War Powers Resolution (WPR) to prevent us from entering a long war with no public support. That's true of the 1973 WPR, but in fact, the AVF had been under consideration since the 1960s, well before the WPR, and its adoption was driven mostly by a desire to find a more economic and effective model for manning the military.

According to the *Oxford Companion to American Military History 2000*:

> The blueprint for the AVF was prepared by President Richard M. Nixon's Commission on an All Volunteer Armed Force, appointed in 1969. Driven by political pressure to end the draft and an ideological commitment to free market forces, the commission headed by Thomas Gates concluded that a volunteer force, supported by the potential to reintroduce the draft, was preferable to a mixed force of conscripts and volunteers, and that, based on labor market dynamics, it was economically feasible to raise a volunteer army.

De Gregorio, to his credit, acknowledges the economic arguments in favor of AVF "were valid," but he focuses on the AVF as the tool for relief from lengthy, unpopular wars.

So many changes were happening in the early 1970s that it is understandable to mistakenly conflate them. Two of those changes are cited by De Gregorio: the War Powers Resolution and the All Volunteer Force. But in fact, the way in which defense planners attempted to prevent long, unpopular wars was not by replacing the draft with a volunteer system but by moving key combat and support functions from the Active component into the Reserves and National Guard. Congress then added the requirement that any lengthy mobilization of these reserves would require the president to get congressional approval. The thinking was that any major war would require the call up of military forces, draft or volunteer, which would in turn involve military members from all the states, not just those with large bases.

In his 2012 *Foreign Policy* article, General Stanley McChrystal also argued for a draft, writing, "I think if a nation goes to war, every town, every city needs to be at risk. You make that decision and everybody has skin in the game." This in fact happened in both Desert Storm (1991) and the wars in Iraq and Afghanistan, because of the 1970s decision to shift forces into the Reserves. For the current wars, which have dragged on for almost two decades, forces from across America in the Reserves and National Guard were needed at such high rates that the Army had to extend troops in the war zones and break dwell time rules back home to meet demand. A visit to any small town in America today will almost certainly reveal a monument or memorial to those from that area who served in the current and recent wars. A draft is not necessary to bring the pain of war to small town America.

A civilian-military disconnect looms over our society.

This is one of the most common complaints about the All Volunteer Force. Preventing or mitigating such a divide has been a concern of the uniformed military since the AVF was instituted in the 1970s, and as a result, leaders have made a concerted effort to reach out to the civilian population. Military units conduct "Open House" days for local populations. They link themselves with local schools and communities by providing support to local events. They form joint community advisory boards to deconflict military base operations and local governments.

Although many civilian and military experts often cite this "divide," there is no real proof of its existence. Neither is there real proof of its negative impact. Simply pointing to the smaller number of troops in the military compared to the Cold War and WWII does not prove that a divide exists between those "proud and few" and the general population.

De Gregorio claimed, "To many, the military are a class of strangers; nameless, faceless beings to whom Americans have no personal attachment. They are an expendable commodity." I suggest that this sentiment more accurately describes the divide between our civilian population and our uniformed military in the 1960s when there was a draft than it does the situation under the All Volunteer Force. The sentiment I experienced during my thirty years of military service was the opposite of the above.

But let us assume, for argument's sake, that there is some kind of divide between those who serve in the military and those who do not. There are many good reasons why such a divide would be in the national interest. A 2013 study commissioned by the Office of the Under Secretary of Defense for Accession Policy found that only 13 percent of America's youth meet the quality standards for service in the military. Excluding 87 percent of American youth from service because they do not qualify could be a divide of sorts, but certainly one that benefits the nation's interest in a strong military.

The most obvious example of a difference between the military and general society is that the military operates under a separate set of laws and regulations. The men and women of the military must be ready to obey any lawful command, even if it could result in their death.

There are many other reasons why the military community lives under different standards and laws. But these differences do not necessarily mean there is a divide between our service members and the general population any more than there is a divide with professional athletes or emergency responders.

Military members are, as a group, proud of the sacrifices they make in service. I wager that most military service members would not trade their strict standards of discipline and conduct for those of the general civilian population; especially because they voluntarily signed up for those standards. And judging by the public support for military service members, any divide, if it exists, is not harmful to the relationship between the military and public. In Gallup's annual Confidence in Institutions poll, the military has topped the list every year since 1998, with at least 72 percent expressing "a great deal" or "quite a lot" of confidence in the military.

> If only in a small way, the DoD's [Department of Defense's] dependence on civilian contractors clearly degrades the cost-savings and efficiencies that served as the basis for transitioning to an AVF.

The proposition that the logistical requirements for our deployed forces could better and more efficiently be served by drafting enough additional troops to address them deserves some investigation. I served in the Army under both the current and previous models and often wondered the same thing. But I do not think the case has been adequately made that the costs would be lower for the same or better quality of logistical support—especially when one considers the numbers of troops, leaders and units required, along with the acquisition and maintenance of the logistical materials needed. For example, the additional downstream costs for retirement and health care for additional troops would have to be figured into the calculations. This rationale certainly should not be a justification for a draft in and of itself.

> The American society's failure to share the burden of a common defense has forced its professional military and their families to pay a volunteer tax that is unsustainable. For the security of the United States, it is time Americans consider instructing their young people that the great benefits of citizenship come with some daunting responsibilities.

The fact that only a few of America's citizens are bearing an outsized burden defending our nation is often cited as a reason why one might consider bringing back a draft. The theory is that a draft would spread the commitment to serve over all strata of society equally: rich, poor, white, non-white, city, rural, etc. Additionally, the draft would somehow involve more young men and women in the military burden than the current system.

But the reason that only a relative few are in the military is not because we have a volunteer system. The reason is that we the people—Congress—have decided that our military should be of a certain size (1.3 million). Congress decides how many troops we can afford to field. Congress decides how many lieutenants, captains, generals, admirals etc. we have—down to the individual person. We have enough volunteers for today's military, but whether we drafted those people into service or accepted them as volunteers, we would still only need 1.3 million service members because that is all that Congress authorizes.

If one thinks we should have more troops in our military, that's a different debate than whether we should get those people through a draft or a volunteer system. But keep in mind that during the 1970s and 1980s when our military was over two million, we did not need a draft to staff that force.

And where do these volunteers come from? From the poor and uneducated of our country? Not at all. According to the FY 2016 report by the Office of the Under Secretary of Defense for Personnel and Readiness, all the recruits accessed into the military scored "considerably higher on the AFQT [an aptitude and education test] than did the 18- to 23-year-old civilian population." The same report showed that the majority of recruits come from middle economic class families: "The findings … are important because they dispel the myth that the military obtains the majority of its recruits from the lower socioeconomic classes—those neighborhoods with the lowest income levels. Quite the opposite is true." Enlisted military members come from all of the fifty states, but some regions contribute more than others. In absolute terms, the top five states for recruitment in 2016 were California, Texas, Florida, Georgia and New York. These statistics demonstrate that the recruits are representative of our nation, while being some of our best young men and women.

> If America fails to return to a conscription model, cultural deterioration will continue, an insufficient number of citizens will answer the call of military duty, and America will not be able to go to war.

Although some military components have difficulty from time to time meeting recruiting goals, over the forty plus years of the AVF the nation's youth have reliably answered the call to serve—whether it was 2.3 million or 1.3 million. Young men and women like Nick De Gregorio have stepped forward to serve their nation in the military. During those forty plus years, America has gone to war numerous times, in both short and extended conflicts. In all those conflicts the vast majority of American military units performed admirably. There is no evidence that there are insufficient volunteers or that America cannot prosecute its wars.

The All Volunteer Force is consistent with American values, in which the government should exercise restraint in circumscribing individual liberty. When there is a good reason to do so, without viable alternatives, such intervention into the lives of citizens is permissible. But if there are alternatives to infringing on personal liberty, both American society and its citizens benefit by allowing individuals to pursue their chosen talents.

Service to one's nation can take many forms: emergency responders, police, teachers, military and others. It should be continuously encouraged among our citizens. But if we mandate service, is it really service? I would rather have a hundred courageous volunteers like Nick De Gregorio than a thousand reluctant warriors.

> *"The more important issue is that forcing anyone to register for Selective Service is unjust because it is based on coercion."*

Forcing Anyone to Register Is Based on Coercion

Jessica Pavoni

In the previous viewpoint, the author argued that a draft is not necessary. In the following viewpoint, author Jessica Pavoni goes a step further to make the case that a draft is not only unnecessary, but immoral. A draft, she says, is a form of slavery. While the author's reasoning applies to men as well as women, she uses the issue of whether or not to draft women as the jumping-off point for her argument. Jessica Pavoni is a writer and former special operations instructor pilot. She has 1,335 combat hours and has been deployed eight times.

"Senate Votes for Equal Slavery for Women: A Female Veteran's Case Against the Selective Service," Jessica Pavoni, Foundation for Economic Education, June 14, 2016. Licensed under CC BY 4.0 International.

As you read, consider the following questions:

1. Why, according to the author, is a draft—for men as well as women—fundamentally unjust?
2. Why does assessing a fine or imprisonment for failure to register for the Selective Service make it "a statute that institutionalizes indentured servitude whenever the government sees fit," according to the viewpoint?
3. The author closes with a quote from Alexis de Tocqueville, the author of *Democracy in America*. How does that quote relate to her premise?

T he *New York Times* reported today: "The United States Senate voted to pass a defense bill today that would require young women to sign up for a potential military draft for the first time in US history."

This issue was bound to come up eventually, as women have recently been allowed to compete for combat positions on the front line. Captain Kristen Griest's recent completion of Army Ranger School and assignment as an Infantry officer is evidence of this shift in both policy and culture.

The accepted logic goes that if women have equal access to all jobs in the military, they ought to have equal responsibility with respect to the draft. And make no mistake: even though there has not been a draft since the 1970s, the ultimate purpose of Selective Service registration is precisely to enable a draft when deemed necessary.

Many are applauding these changes as an important step towards "equality" and recognition of women's capabilities. But the focus on equality is masking the underlying injustice of the law in the first place. The more important issue is that forcing *anyone* to register for Selective Service is unjust because it is based on coercion (and has the potential to place otherwise peaceful people into violent situations). Let's examine why.

How a Draft Would Work

The last American was drafted in 1973. Nevertheless, the Selective Service continues to be funded at about $23 million a year, and there are about 100 people in the US who's job it is to be at the ready just in case.

Many work at Selective Service headquarters at Arlington, Virginia, which is also home to "The Machine."

On a recent Wednesday, Vince McClure, a program analyst at the Selective Service, wheeled it out so our photographer could take a look. The machine is actually two, clear, fish-tank-like hexagons manufactured by Garron, the same company that makes the devices used by a lot of state lottos.

Every month, McClure or one of his colleagues rolls out the machine, boots it up, and makes sure it'd be ready to jump into action, should duty call.

The first machine has white ping pong balls—the "precedence number," McClure explains. "With numbers from one to 366. And the other has blue balls in it, with the dates of January 1 to December 31."

Those are the birthdays.

In each machine, the racks drop balls into the tank and they mix, until one rolls into the tube. Each birthday gets paired with a precedence number.

If this were a real draft, the Selective Service would come for 20-year-olds first. So if you're 20 years old, and your birthday pops up at the same time as precedence number one, that means you.

Next up would be: 21, 22, 23, 24-year-olds.

Then, the 18 and 19-year-olds.

And finally the draft would apply to 25 and 26-year-olds.

If someone is enrolled in an undergraduate degree program at the time they're drafted, the student would be allowed to finish their current semester—then, they'd have to leave school for induction into the armed forces. But if the student is in their senior year of undergraduate studies at the time they're drafted, they'd be allowed to finish and graduate no matter which semester they're in.

Whether women would be included in any future draft is up in the air.

"Here's How a Modern Military Draft Would Work," by John Ismay, Southern California Public Radio, October 13, 2015.

Penalties for Failing to Register with Selective Service

Most people are aware that failing to register with Selective Service makes a man ineligible for federal student financial aid, and seriously impacts his ability to get a government job, obtain a security clearance, or gain citizenship. Fine, you may say—a young man who does not want to register can pay the price by not pursuing federal financial aid, and not getting a government job, security clearance, or applying for citizenship. That is a fair trade, and at least there is no violation of natural rights in that scenario; all a man needs to do is exercise his right to opt out or disassociate. But there's more:

> Failing to register or comply with the Military Selective Service Act is a felony punishable by a fine of up to $250,000 or a prison term of up to five years, or a combination of both. Also, a person who knowingly counsels, aids, or abets another to fail to comply with the Act is subject to the same penalties. (Selective Service System)

And there you have it—where the law is exposed for what it really is: a statute that institutionalizes indentured servitude whenever the government sees fit. That is exactly what military service is, whether you join voluntarily or are conscripted into the armed forces. Now if you refuse to register, your entire professional life is likely to be destroyed. Any person who recognizes the principle of self-ownership will immediately understand why requiring a person to register for the draft is the antithesis of personal freedom. If you fail to register, you risk your liberty (through jail time) or the fruits of your labor (by paying a fine) for committing no crime at all. There is no reason to believe that if women are made to register for Selective Service that these penalties will change—and they will infringe on women's rights the same way that they currently infringe on men's rights.

No Great Step for Women

This article is not meant to doubt the ability of women to perform physically demanding tasks in dangerous, high-stakes environments. Indeed, women have been successfully engaged in many different roles during war for decades, as medics, pilots, gunners, Female Engagement Team members, and more. Unfortunately, many people have been pining for "equal" treatment for women without considering what the actual *treatment* is—and whether it's a good thing for men, either.

The real issue at play with this latest amendment is not whether women can or should fill combat roles, and thereby be eligible for the draft. The real issue is that a Selective Service registration (which leads to a draft) is immoral for both men *and* women, and that neither should be required to register at risk of becoming a felon, being fined, or being put in jail. The mere presence of a draft registration is an assertion that some people are qualified to put other people's lives at risk. They aren't.

Moreover, an important point is missing from the national discussion: if the United States were actually to be attacked, there would be no shortage of volunteers to defend the country. Instead, a draft would most likely be utilized to fight a war in which willing volunteers were hard to find…which is perhaps a damning indictment of the motives for a particular war.

While many are hailing Selective Service registration as a step forward for women, I am rather reminded of these wise words from Alexis de Tocqueville: "Americans are so enamored of equality that they would rather be equal in slavery than unequal in freedom."

> "The past 30 years—and particularly
> the experience in Iraq and
> Afghanistan—demonstrate that
> an All-Volunteer Armed Force can
> be sustained during both peace
> and war."

There Are Many Significant Advantages to an All-Volunteer Military

Bernard D. Rostker

Here, we take a step back and hear from an author who gives a historical and social background of the draft in the United States and of the development of the all-volunteer military. In the following viewpoint, Bernard Rostker ultimately argues in favor of an all-volunteer force. However, in making his case he takes a slightly different approach to some of the arguments detailed in the previous two viewpoints. Bernard Rostker is a senior fellow of the RAND Corporation. He served as director of the US Selective Service System from 1979 to 1981.

"The Evolution of the All-Volunteer Force," by Bernard D. Rostker, RAND Corporation, July 17, 2016. Reprinted by permission.

As you read, consider the following questions:

1. What reasons does the author list for the change in Americans' attitudes about the draft?
2. In what ways has the all-volunteer military improved the US armed forces, according to the author?
3. What effect did the end of the Cold War have upon military planning and the need for a draft?

In 1969, four years before the United States eliminated the draft and moved to an all-volunteer force, a member of the President's Commission on an All-Volunteer Armed Force wrote to its chairman that "while there is a reasonable possibility that a peacetime armed force could be entirely voluntary, I am certain that an armed force involved in a major conflict could not be voluntary."[1] So far, his reservations have not been borne out. However, given the ongoing war in Iraq—with casualties rising, enlistments dropping, and a majority of the American public no longer believing that the war is worth fighting—the issue of recruiting enough volunteers to maintain the US military at required levels is again relevant.

I Want You! The Evolution of the All-Volunteer Force provides a richly detailed history that begins in the 1960s, when the credibility of the draft was called into serious question, and ends in the present, when long overseas deployments and the deteriorating situation in Iraq may adversely affect the sustainability of the all-volunteer system. The author, Bernard Rostker, is a senior RAND fellow with four decades of experience as both a policy analyst and policymaker in the area of defense manpower. Drawing on a vast archive of US government materials, including many recently declassified documents, he addresses the complexities of the subject by alternating chapters that describe the key historical and political events of each period with corresponding chapters that focus on the research that has been used to inform the decision making process.

In the foreword to this book, former Secretary of Defense Melvin Laird observes that "the work constitutes a virtual archive of the many events, issues, facets, and fundamentals constituting the all-volunteer force. The research and documentation exceed by far, in my judgment, any prior attempts to explore this subject." Thus, it is an extremely valuable resource for scholars and students of military affairs and public administration.

Why Did the United States Move to an All-Volunteer Force (AVF)?

Although the country had conscripted its armed forces for only 35 of its 228 years—nearly all in the 20th century—the American people were generally willing to accept this practice when service was perceived as universal. However, in the 1960s, that acceptance began to erode. There were five major reasons:

- **Demographics.** The size of the eligible population of young men reaching draft age each year was so large and the needs of the military so small in comparison that, in practice, the draft was no longer universal.
- **Cost.** Obtaining enough volunteers was possible at acceptable budget levels.
- **Moral and economic rationale.** Conservatives and libertarians argued that the state had no right to impose military service on young men without their consent. Liberals asserted that the draft placed unfair burdens on the underprivileged members of society, who were less likely to get deferments.
- **Opposition to the war in Vietnam.** The growing unpopularity of the Vietnam War meant the country was ripe for a change to a volunteer force.
- **The US Army's desire for change.** The Army had lost confidence in the draft as discipline problems among draftees mounted in Vietnam.

These views were reinforced by the findings of the Gates Commission, set up in 1969 by President Richard Nixon to advise him on establishing an all-volunteer force. The commission addressed key military-manpower issues, including supply and demand, attrition and retention, and the mix of career and noncareer members in the context of management efficiency and personal equity. It concluded that the nation's interests would be better served by an all-volunteer force than by a combination of volunteers and conscripts. In 1971, President Nixon signed a new law to end the draft and put the selective service structure on standby. After a two-year extension of induction authority, the end of the draft was formally announced in January 1973.

Effective Use of Research Has Been Instrumental in Establishing the AVF

Since 1964, personnel managers have used research to help develop, implement, and sustain the AVF. The research has been policy relevant, and the mixture of different disciplines—economics, psychology, social psychology, and sociology—produced a comprehensive and credible assessment of alternative policies.

The research of the 1960s and early 1970s reassured decision makers that an AVF might be possible at acceptable budget outlays. In the 1970s and 1980s, various test programs demonstrated the value of advertising and the benefits of educational incentives and bonuses in encouraging enlistment. Analytical evidence supported the need to reform the compensation system. Studies of accession testing and job performance proved what now seems so logical but was once very controversial: People who score higher on standardized tests do better on the job than those who score lower. The resulting emphasis on quality attracted capable people and led to increasing professionalism within the military services. A largely unexpected consequence of moving to a professional military with better pay was the higher rate of reenlistment and a sharp increase in the size of the career force.

Since the fall of the Soviet Union in 1989 and the disappearance of the threat that had dominated national security strategy for half a century, personnel research has helped managers make the adjustments that were needed to transition the larger post–Cold War military to a smaller, more-agile, and more-engaged force.

The AVF Has Changed the Military for the Better

Since the establishment of the AVF, the quality of the force, measured by scores on standardized IQ tests, has improved. The percentage of new recruits with high school diplomas has increased. The AVF has dramatically increased the number of career personnel and increased the proficiency and professionalism of the force.

The AVF is also broadly representative of the American people. For the past 26 years, the Department of Defense has annually reported on social representation in the US military. The 2004 report noted the following:

- **Age.** The active-duty population is younger than the overall civilian sector. Forty-nine percent of the active-duty force is between the ages of 17 and 24, whereas about 15 percent of the civilian workforce falls between those ages. Similarly, officers are younger than their civilian counterparts.
- **Gender.** Today, 15 percent of the active-duty enlisted force is female, compared with less than 2 percent when the draft ended. Sixteen percent of the officer corps is female. Despite these improvements, women are still underrepresented in the military.
- **Marital status.** The larger career force means that the number of service members who are married has increased. Today, 49 percent of enlisted personnel are married, compared with 40 percent at the start of the AVF. Sixty-eight percent of all active-duty officers are married.
- **Educational level.** The most recent statistics show that 92 percent of the new accessions to the active-duty force are high school graduates. The figure for the reserve components is 87 percent. This is a dramatic increase from the 1973 goal

of 45 percent and today's goal of 79 percent. In addition, 95 percent of active-duty officers have baccalaureate degrees, and 38 percent have advanced degrees.

- **Socioeconomic status.** Recruits come primarily from families in the middle or lower middle classes. The high end of the distribution is not well represented.
- **Race and ethnicity.** In fiscal year 2002, African-Americans were slightly overrepresented among new enlisted accessions relative to the civilian population: 16 percent compared with 14 percent. However, this is considerably below the 1973 level of 28 percent. Hispanics are underrepresented, making up 16 percent of all civilians but only 11 percent of new accessions.

The Success of the AVF Depends on Four Factors

Reflecting on 30 years' experience with the AVF suggests four broad reasons for its success. The first is attention and leadership from top management. The AVF would not have come about when it did without the leadership of President Nixon. Within weeks of taking office in 1969, he began the planning process and announced the formation of the Gates Commission. Secretary of Defense Melvin Laird (under Nixon) and Secretary of Defense Caspar Weinberger (in the early 1980s, under President Ronald Reagan) were likewise among the senior government officials who provided strong support for the AVF. Turning to the military, Army General Maxwell Thurman is considered by many as the single most important person in the history of the AVF because he taught the Pentagon how to recruit and, by dint of personality and intellect, made the AVF concept work throughout the 1980s.

A second contributing factor is the use of quantitative analysis to test, adjust, and evaluate AVF policies. Well-designed, policy-relevant research to measure job performance and determine the optimum mix of quality and cost has resulted in the proficient and committed AVF that now serves the nation.

Third is the need to develop programs for attracting the necessary type and number of recruits. The AVF's focus on quality has already been discussed here. To attract high-quality youths, the services had to develop appropriate marketing strategies and advertising programs that explained the benefits and opportunities of military service. The military learned that it had to offer money for education, bonuses to enlist in certain occupations, and enlistment tours of different lengths. It needed to develop career opportunities that had civilian relevance and were a good preparation for adulthood. The services also had to develop a professional, highly trained, and motivated recruiting staff. Finally, reenlisting the most capable members was the key to creating a truly outstanding force. Besides good pay, careerists demanded quality-of-life benefits such as good housing, child care, health benefits, family advocacy programs, and military stores. It was crucial that the services become "family friendly."

The fourth factor is adequate financial resources. The defense budget must be large enough to support pay raises that keep pace with both inflation and civilian-sector pay increases; to provide resources for advertising, recruiters, bonuses, and educational benefits; and to fund the military retirement program and quality-of-life initiatives.

What Does the Future Hold for the AVF?

Today, with nearly 160,000 troops engaged in Iraq and Afghanistan, the AVF is being tested again. Military commanders continually point to the outstanding job the force is doing in this nontraditional military conflict. Remarkably, while enlistments have fallen off, retention remains at historically high levels. There were initial fears that soldiers would not reenlist if they had to redeploy even once into combat zones. However, the Army reports that some soldiers are now completing their third and fourth tours. Through improved pay and benefits for the military, America has demonstrated that it values an AVF. Our troops have likewise demonstrated their commitment through their willingness to serve.

A final judgment on the AVF has not yet been made. Indeed, it will always be a work in progress. However, the past 30 years—and particularly the experience in Iraq and Afghanistan—demonstrate that an AVF can be sustained during both peace and war. The dual challenges of longer periods of conflict and recurring deployments are formidable. There are no guarantees of permanent success. But, so far, the AVF has proven to be a resilient institution.

Notes

1. Crawford H. Greenewalt, memorandum to Thomas Gates, Wilmington, Delaware, December 31, 1969.

> *"These recruits, whether conscripts or volunteers, were 'citizen-soldiers,' whose attachment to their societies and stake in their states' existence go far to explain the tremendous resilience of the armies of 1914–18."*

Conscripts as Well as Volunteers Can Be Motivated by Patriotism

Alexander Watson

So far, the viewpoints in this chapter have focused mostly on the draft from a United States-centered perspective. In the following viewpoint, Alexander Watson looks at World War I and takes an international view. The author begins by explaining how conscription began and worked in Europe. Then he discusses the differences between volunteers and conscripts. He concludes that both groups were valuable "citizen soldiers." Alexander Watson is a scholar at the University of London. He specializes in the history of Britain and East-Central Europe during World War I.

"Recruitment: Conscripts and Volunteers During World War One," by Alexander Watson, January 29, 2014. © British Library Board.

As you read, consider the following questions:

1. How does the conscription method described here differ from those discussed in previous viewpoints?
2. What does the author say was the primary motivation for both volunteers and conscripts at this time?
3. What, according to the viewpoint, accounts for the great resiliency of soldiers during World War I?

T he First World War was fought predominantly by conscript armies fielding millions of "citizen-soldiers." The origins of this type of military lay in the *levée en masse* (mass mobilisation) organised by the French revolutionary regime at the end of the 18th century, the first modern force built on the idea that all male citizens had a duty to bear arms in defence of their nation. However, it was France's rival Prussia which improved and systemised the military model, developing a new form of universal short-service peacetime conscription. After spectacular victories over Austria and France in 1866 and 1871, this provided the organisational template for other continental European armies. Austria-Hungary imitated it in 1868, France in 1872 and Russia in 1874. Britain and the United States, which relied primarily on their navies for security, were alone among the major powers in remaining with small professional armies.

How Conscription Worked

Short-service systems of conscription obliged healthy male citizens to undergo a relatively brief period of military training in their youth and then made them subject for much of the rest of their adult lives to call up for refresher courses or for service in an emergency. The exact terms of service varied from country to country but Germany's system provides a good example. There, men were drafted at age 20 for two or three years of peacetime training in the active army. While all had an obligation to serve, financial limitations meant in practice that only a little over half of each male year group was conscripted. After training, men were released into civilian life but could be called back to the army until they reached the age of 45. In between, men passed through various reserve categories. Those who had most recently completed their training belonged to the first-line reserve for five years, where they could expect to be redrafted early in the event of crisis. Later, they were allocated for a decade to the second-line *Landwehr*. The third-line *Landsturm* was the oldest band of reservists, intended mainly for rear-line duties in a major war. The short-service conscript system offered two major advantages. First, it created a large pool of trained manpower that could quickly augment the standing army in an emergency. In August 1914, the German army needed just 12 days to expand from 808,280 to 3,502,700 soldiers. Second, in a long conflict, the system offered an organisational framework capable of deploying nearly the entire manpower of a state as soldiers. Conscript forces became true "nations in arms" in 1914–18. 55% of male Italians and Bulgarians aged 18 to 50 were called to military service. Elsewhere the proportions were even higher: 63% of military-aged men in Serbia, 78% in Austro-Hungary and 81% of military-aged men in France and Germany served.

War Volunteers and Enlistment Motivations

While conscript armies proved indispensable, and even the British in 1916 and the Americans in 1917 began to draft men, significant numbers of volunteers also served in the First World War. Most famously, in Britain 2,675,149 men volunteered, the vast majority in the first half of hostilities. However, even countries with long traditions of conscription also had large volunteering movements. In Germany, around half a million men came forward. The great rush was at the start of the war: in the first 10 days 143,922 men enlisted in Prussian units alone. France's voluntary enlistments were smaller but steadier, reaching 187,905 men by the end of hostilities. In multinational Austria-Hungary, men appear to have been less willing to volunteer for the Emperor's army, although they promptly obeyed call up orders. Some nationalist movements did recruit successfully, however. The Polish Legionaries, the largest of these forces, had 21,000 volunteers by 1917. While volunteers tended to be disproportionately middle-class, their motives for joining the army may not have been so different from those of conscripts. Patriotic duty appears to have been a prime motivation for both groups, although coercion was also influential. Volunteers were not subject to the legal sanctions faced by conscripts who disobeyed drafting orders but they might be exposed to considerable social pressure to enlist. For small minorities, economic factors or lust for action and adventure were important. These recruits, whether conscripts or volunteers, were "citizen-soldiers," whose attachment to their societies and stake in their states' existence go far to explain the tremendous resilience of the armies of 1914–18.

| "*Long wars become possible because the boots-on-the-ground can be deployed and redeployed.*"

An All-Volunteer Military Makes It Easier to Go to War

Jeff Shear

Previous viewpoints have argued that an all-volunteer military is more efficient, better motivated, and generally better at its job. This, they seemed to be saying, was a good thing. In the following viewpoint, Jeff Shear argues precisely the opposite, that a professional military makes it easier for the country to get involved in wars without adequate input from the public. Jeff Shear is a journalist, author, and former fellow at the Center for Public Integrity in Washington, DC.

As you read, consider the following questions:

1. In what crucial way, according to the viewpoint, does a professional or volunteer military differ from a military made up of draftees?
2. What reasons does the author give to support his claim that a standing, professional military makes it easier for Washington to go to war?
3. What, according to the viewpoint, is the disadvantage of drawing military recruits mostly from military families?

"America in the Hands of a Professional Military," by Jeff Shear, The Social Justice Foundation, June 14, 2017. Reprinted by permission.

Americans observe two anniversaries this year, neither one of them wanted. March marked eight years of combat in Iraq, and October, 10 years of fighting in Afghanistan. These are America's "long wars," a seemingly endless grind of combat.

These long wars invite comparison, and some recall the eight years of US war in Vietnam, but there is a more compelling distinction. It was a conscript Army that flew its Hueys over the jungles of the Mekong Delta; it is an all-volunteer force that drives its Humvees along the Tigris and in the shattered urban landscape of Kabul.

For nearly 40 years, these volunteers have defended the United States' national interests, and over time they have changed the nation's approach to warfare, foreign policy, domestic politics and even national character. Most often, these affects appear to be subtle, like the growing distance between the military and the civilian population, or the percentage of Americans who have relatives in the services. Still, the consequences have been profound, making it easier for the US to go to war with little public scrutiny.

The plans for this standing military were drawn up in 1969. The Big Think work was done by the President's Commission on an All-Volunteer Force, which came to be known as the Gates Commission after its chairman, Thomas S. Gates, Jr., an investment banker and former defense secretary. Nixon received the commission's report in February 1970. And little more than three years later, in June 1973, the last man drafted into the US military reported for training.

The volunteers followed. While it's true that many young men and women have chosen to enlist for the four years of training, educational incentives and an $8,000 bonus, America has never had so large a standing military. At the dawn of World War II, the US Army and National Guard was 400,000 strong, plus another 125,000 in the Navy; the Gates Commission 30 years later planned for a force "somewhere between 2,000,000 and 3,000,000 men." The volunteer force conceived in the 1970s to fight the Cold War has grown into a military geared to fighting what Army Chief of

Staff George W. Casey, Jr. calls an era of "persistent conflict." And that has turned a force of amateurs into professionals.

The distinction between volunteer and professional is crucial, because it best "... captures the significance of the changes that we've undergone in our approach to military policy since Vietnam," says historian and Boston University professor Andrew Bacevich, a retired career Army colonel.

"The military is far more professional and capable than ever before," says Col. Lance Betros, the head of the history department at the United States Military Academy at West Point. "There's a big difference between what we have now and anything we've had before."

Most important, the soldiers agree. They see themselves as professionals, as the recent documentary film *Restrepo* makes clear. Preparing for a deadly showdown with the Taliban in Afghanistan's Korengal Valley, the soldiers psych for battle, telling themselves they are "professional tough guys."

These professional tough guys have had a direct and perhaps shocking effect on foreign policy, says Thomas Keaney, director of the Philip Merrill Center for Strategic Studies at Johns Hopkins University. "They make it easier for Washington to go to war. You don't need a special congressional action or the threat of a draft to send in the troops."

The professional military also makes it possible to sustain wars. Long wars become possible because the boots-on-the-ground can be deployed and redeployed. In the past, to fight wars like the ones in Afghanistan and Iraq, "you would have had to institute a draft in order to sustain the action that's been going on," Keaney says. "And that would have been a brake on any administration."

Vietnam is a vivid example of an administration hitting the brakes. In 1968, the draft focused public attention on the war. Protests shook the nation. Young people publicly burned their draft cards, and in a stunning about-face in domestic politics, President Lyndon Johnson declined to seek a second term in office.

Persistent Conflict

But the professional military has taken the public out of the mix, something noted at the highest levels of government. Speaking at Duke University in September, Secretary of Defense Robert Gates (no relation to Thomas) noted the disconnect: "Whatever their fond sentiments for men and women in uniform, for most Americans the wars [in Iraq and Afghanistan] remain an abstraction. A distant and unpleasant series of news items that does not affect them personally ... warfare has become something for other people to do."

Bacevich goes further. "Americans," he said, "have forfeited any real sense of ownership or responsibility for the defense of the United States. One consequence of that is they have far less say over where and how US forces are deployed. To an enormously large extent, Washington makes the decisions about where and how to deploy US forces, and public opinion doesn't matter in any significant way."

How does the public actually think about the military? The venerable Gallup Organization has queried this issue over the decade. It regularly asks the public to rate its institutions, and year after year, their polls show Americans have more confidence in the military than any other institution.

The public holds the military in high esteem, even "though warfare has become something for other people to do," as Secretary Gates pointed out. A 2008 USA Today/Gallup poll found that two-thirds of Americans see service in the military as patriotic.

But the public is less sure about sending its own children into combat. In 1999, the Associated Press asked parents if they would support their children if they wished to enter the military. More than 70 percent of respondents said they would support their children if they elected to go into service.

Six years later, after 9/11 and after Iraq, Gallup asked the same question. This time, less than half of the respondents said they would support their child's choice to go into the military. "This reluctance to support a military career is not a reflection on the military itself," Gallup reported. "... A more likely explanation probably lies in the realization that military service is more dangerous today given the ongoing war in Iraq."

Echoing this explanation for this public change of heart is an Associated Press/Roper Poll taken late last summer. Nearly two-thirds of respondents opposed the war (65 percent) and solidly more than half opposed the war in Afghanistan (58 percent).

Secretary Gates described part of the phenomenon when he said, "Warfare has become something for other people to do." It does not affect them "personally," until a loved one goes to war.

Take Matthew Dowd, chief strategist for the 2004 Bush-Cheney re-election campaign and a major force in Republican circles. In March 2007, he left his job, disillusioned with the war in Iraq. He then had "skin in the game"—his son was about to deploy to Iraq as an Army intelligence specialist.

"If you have skin in the game—your investment is greater," says Lt. Col. Brenda Cartier, the first woman to command a squadron of covert operations AC-130U "Spooky" gun ships. She has spent five-and-a-half of the last 10 years in combat roles.

A great concern when the Gates Commission worked out the arguments in favor of an all-volunteer military was that the resulting force would become "ghettoized." The commission worried that "(1) an all-volunteer force will become isolated from society and threaten civilian control; (2) isolation and alienation will erode civilian respect for the military and hence dilute its quality; (3) an all-volunteer force will be all-black or dominated by servicemen from low-income backgrounds; (4) an all-volunteer force will lead to a decline in patriotism or in popular concern about foreign policy; (5) an all-volunteer force will encourage military adventurism."

That seems prescient. The percentage of forces enlisting from the populous Northeast, the West Coast and the big cities is in decline, according to Gates. What is more, the volunteers who do sign on are not from the wider public, but people who already have connections to the armed services. Most troops have grown up in or around military families, much like Cartier, whose grandfathers, father, brother and uncles all served in the Army, the Air Force or the Marines.

That sense of belonging has served the military well in these persistent conflicts. As the RAND Corporation noted in a research brief on the all-volunteer force, "Military commanders continually point to the outstanding job the force is doing in this nontraditional military conflict. Remarkably, while enlistments have fallen off, retention remains at historically high levels."

Meanwhile, the military has also grown physically remote from the wider public. Basing changes have moved a significant percentage of Army posts to just five states—Texas, Washington, Kentucky, Georgia and North Carolina. As Gates put it, the military is a "tiny sliver of America," significantly less than 1 percent of the population.

Because of the professional nature of the military, fewer and fewer Americans are connected to these long wars or to the military itself. "With each passing decade fewer and fewer Americans know someone with military experience in their family or social circle," according to Secretary Gates. According to one study he cited, in 1988 about 40 percent of 18-year-olds had a veteran parent. By 2000, the share had dropped to 18 percent, and is projected to continue falling.

West Point's Lance Betros adds: "The military is losing contact with the wider society. And those who make the decisions about military force really don't have any skin in the fight. We've reached the point where you have to wonder how well policy makers understand the consequences of their actions when it comes to national deterrence."

When the Gates Commission signed off on its report, the 91st Congress had nearly 400 veterans, from World War II and Korea. The just completed 111th Congress had far fewer, 121. Only seven members of the 110th Congress had family serving in Iraq or Afghanistan.

The fear is not that the military would attempt to usurp the government. "The real danger," Betros says, "is that Americans reflexively move towards a military solution before they will try all the other elements of national power. For now, the country relies very, very heavily on its military, without asking if there is an alternative. When all you have is a hammer, every problem looks like a nail."

"A national service program should augment the current all-volunteer US military. This will foster a culture of universal contribution among citizens and prevent the emergence of a society so internally fractured that it lacks the will and ability to assert itself against America's many external threats."

America Should Have Compulsory Military Service

Nick De Gregorio

In the following viewpoint, Nick De Gregorio argues that the United States should have compulsory military service. Like several previous viewpoint authors, De Gregorio argues that an all-volunteer military separates the public from the military, but his reasons for thinking this a bad thing are slightly different. The author contends that the problem with an all-volunteer military is that it weakens the collective will to take part in defending and caring for the nation. His solution? A compulsory national service program to augment the military. Nick De Gregorio is a 2018 graduate of Georgetown University's Master of Science in Foreign Service (MSFS) and Master of Business Administration (MBA) programs. He is a veteran of the wars in Iraq and Afghanistan.

"Draft Time: This Is Why and How America Should Have Compulsory Military Service," by Nick De Gregorio, Center for the National Interest, August 14, 2018. Reprinted by permission.

As you read, consider the following questions:

1. What was the 1973 War Powers Resolution and why was it enacted?
2. In what way has Congress abdicated its responsibility regarding the country's involvement in wars?
3. What is the Ricks Plan for national service, and what does the author see as the pros and cons of it?

1 973 was a pivotal year in American history. After nearly a decade of direct military involvement, the last remaining US combat troops returned home from Vietnam. While the war would carry on for two more years, with US advisors trying in vain to stave off the fall of Saigon, many at home breathed a deep sigh of relief that America's then-longest conflict was coming to an end.

"Never again" best embodies the Spirit of '73. Through the 1973 War Powers Resolution (WPR), the United States committed to never again enable the President to prosecute lengthy wars without the express consent of Congress. Additionally, through the 1973 implementation of the All-Volunteer Force (AVF), we committed to never again draft our young men and women into military service. Vietnam had shown Americans the error of their ways, and they corrected their deficiencies accordingly.

The problem is, neither of these "fixes" actually fixed anything. Congress routinely abdicates its responsibility to check the executive branch's protracted use of military force abroad, as is demonstrated by a conflict in Afghanistan now in its seventeenth year without a formal declaration of war. Also, while AVF implementation has enabled America to sustain its military pre-eminence, this achievement has come at a significant cultural cost.

A civilian-military disconnect looms over our society. The share of the US population with military experience is at an all-time low, with a scant 7.3 percent of living Americans have served in the military at some point in their lives. This means fewer parents of troops, siblings of troops, spouses of troops, and friends of troops. To many, the military are a class of strangers; nameless, faceless beings to whom Americans have no personal attachment. They are an expendable commodity. Well-intentioned as the AVF transition may have been during a time of great national introspection, time has revealed the long-term cultural limitations of such a model.

A correction to the post-Vietnam over-correction is due. Defense of America and its ideals must be made collective again, lest Americans become culturally over-reliant on a small, professional soldiery that shares increasingly fewer social commonalities with the people it is charged with defending. A national service program should augment the current all-volunteer US military. This will foster a culture of universal contribution among citizens and prevent the emergence of a society so internally fractured that it lacks the will and ability to assert itself against America's many external threats.

But before the critiques are considered, here are some concessions. Most economists agree that the AVF is (ceteris paribus, of course) superior to a conscription model. Conscription generally ignores the opportunity costs of those citizens who could earn higher wages doing something else, which reduces the tax base and increases the net US tax burden. Under conscription, the state must expend resources to mitigate the evasion of those who do not wish to serve. Furthermore, conscripts tend to serve shorter terms and re-enlist at lower rates than volunteers, leading to cost inefficiencies over time. The lower wage rate associated with a draft system also creates an environment whereby cheap, labor-intensive conscripts are used as a replacement for capital-intensive technological improvements, trading long-term efficiency for short-term savings. These were some of the justifications made in 1973 by the many economists advising the Nixon administration to end the draft, and they are valid arguments.

It is unlikely, however, that these economists could have foreseen the US military's staggering dependence on civilian contractors to facilitate war in the twenty-first century. The United States Army established the Logistical Civil Augmentation Program (LOGCAP) in 1985, with an original purpose of providing regional unified commanders the flexibility to meet supply and service requirements unique to their specific areas of command. What was once a means of funding local, one-off construction projects in far-away corners of the globe has metastasized into a DoD process for awarding comprehensive high-dollar combat service support contracts to private sector firms.

The first such comprehensive contract, LOGCAP I (1992–1997), saw the provision of $824 million in logistical support for US military operations overseas. In the wake of the September 11 attacks, as force projection requirements grew, so did LOGCAP expenditures. At the peak of the Global War on Terror (GWOT) in 2008, $150 billion in defense spending was allocated to private sector firms over ten years through LOGCAP IV. Even today, as the major conflicts in Iraq and Afghanistan have drawn down considerably, solicitation for the $82 billion, ten-year LOGCAP V contract is underway.

Numerous cases of fraud, waste, and abuse have plagued the LOGCAP program. In 2007, the DoD created the independent Commission on Army Acquisition and Program Management in Expeditionary Operations, whose findings called for urgent LOGCAP reform. The commission recommended complete organizational restructuring, legislative oversight, and better training and equipment for both military and civilian contracting personnel.

If only in a small way, the DoD's dependence on civilian contractors clearly degrades the cost-savings and efficiencies that served as the basis for transitioning to an AVF. But in a much larger way, the cultural costs of this complete AVF transition are beginning to reveal themselves through the lingering wear and tear of the GWOT.

Due to the smaller size of the US volunteer military force, operations tempo has increased at an alarming rate to meet theater personnel needs with a limited pool of professional troops. The typical deployment requirement for a Vietnam War draftee was one twelve-month tour of duty. Troops serving multiple tours in Vietnam were rare. In contrast, volunteers for the Iraq and Afghanistan wars sustained an average of 1.72 tours of duty over the course of the conflicts. Of those who deployed, 43 percent did so more than once. Dwell times between tours of duty averaged 21 months for all service branches, with active duty Marines operating on a measly 15.76 months of time at home with family before going off into harm's way all over again.

It should come as no surprise, then, that the reintegration challenges faced by new veterans have become an epidemic of national concern. Suicide rates among GWOT service members are 20% to 25% higher than their civilian counterparts. GWOT service members are committing suicide at higher rates than Vietnam veterans did when they returned home from war. Divorce rates among GWOT veterans appear to correlate positively with deployment frequency. This says nothing of the strain placed on those non-marital relationships that cannot be quantified. The American society's failure to share the burden of a common defense has forced its professional military and their families to pay a volunteer tax that is unsustainable.

Equally worrisome are the deleterious cultural effects the AVF has had on the civilian populace. In 2015, as the Islamic State (IS) gained strength in the Middle East and demonstrated its ability to perpetrate high-profile terror attacks in Europe, 60 percent of American survey respondents aged 18 to 29 expressed support for redeploying US ground troops to Iraq. Yet when asked if they would serve should additional troops be needed to fight IS, 85 percent stated they would not or probably would not volunteer. The *Washington Post* presented this data with the blunt-but-true headline: "Millennials embrace a long-standing tradition: Letting someone else fight their wars." Meanwhile, with little fanfare, the DoD stated earlier this year that there may not be enough of "someone else" to sustain the AVF for much longer. For the security of the United States, it is time Americans consider instructing their young people that the great benefits of citizenship come with some daunting responsibilities. It is time America instituted a national service program to save Americans from themselves.

But how? The topic of national service program implementation has been exhaustively debated. A well-known conscription plan presented by Thomas Ricks in 2012 has been criticized for its abridgement of young people's freedom, and the likelihood that its implementation will be viewed as an affront to the increasingly accepted notion that entitlements are inalienable rights. Ricks' plan should be criticized (more on that soon), but not for these reasons. In fact, it is these seemingly anti-conscription arguments that affirm the need to return to a conscription model. Americans have come to expect safety, self-determination, and entitlements on the backs of others. The only way to reverse this suicidal cultural fallacy is to foster a society that understands freedom is not free.

The flaws in Ricks' plan are nested in the intent of his proposal. Ricks' interest in conscription was ultimately singular: halting US military adventurism. If more American moms and dads are required to send their kids off to die for their country, America's collective interest in conflict will abate, the United States will go to war less, and America will be better off. This thought process is noble and probably true, but it misses the existential mark.

If America fails to return to a conscription model, cultural deterioration will continue, an insufficient number of citizens will answer the call of military duty, and America will not be able to go to war. A national service program should not be implemented simply to limit US involvement abroad (noble as that end may be), but to ensure that America possesses in perpetuity the ability to involve itself abroad when it is in the national interest.

Intent aside, Ricks' plan offers a viable national service program blueprint. High school graduates would have three avenues from which to choose: military service, civilian national service, or no service. The first two options would offer positive incentives such as college tuition assistance, medical care, and mortgage guarantees. Opting out of national service would be perfectly legal, but would come with the negative incentive of foregoing many of the entitlement benefits Americans have come to expect as part-and-parcel to citizenship. Perhaps superior plans will materialize in the future as America comes to terms with its inability to defend itself. For now, the Ricks Plan seems like a pretty good place to start.

Now is the time to implement a national service program. China no longer feigns friendship and has made its hegemonic intentions known. Russia continues to test amid the backdrop of a North Atlantic Treaty Organization alliance that has seen much happier times. Alliances are vital, but fleeting. In the end, a nation-state can only truly rely on itself to ensure its interests. France, Sweden, and many other European nations have come to terms with this reality and returned to a national service model. While Americans should endeavor never to go it alone, American citizens must be prepared to heed the old Roman maxim: Si vis pacem, para bellum. That goes for everyone.

Periodical and Internet Sources Bibliography

The following articles have been selected to supplement the diverse views presented in this chapter.

Elliot Ackerman, "Why Bringing Back the Draft Could Stop America's Forever Wars," *Time*, October 10, 2019. https://time .com/5696950/bring-back-the-draft/

Doug Bandow, "Universal Mandatory National Service: A Dystopian Vision for a Free Society," Cato Institute, February 21, 2019. https://www.cato.org/publications/testimony/mandatory -universal-national-service-dystopian-vision-free-society

Charli Carpenter, "America Needs a National Service Draft Now to Fight the Coronavirus," *Foreign Policy*, April 7, 2020. https:// foreignpolicy.com/2020/04/07/america-needs-national-civilian -service-draft-to-fight-coronavirus/

Steve Cohen, "Hard Times in America Renew the Call for National Mandatory Service," *The Hill,* April 22, 2020. https://thehill.com /opinion/national-security/493178-hard-times-in-america -renew-the-call-for-mandatory-national-service

Conor Friedersdorf, "The Case Against Universal National Service," *The Atlantic*, June 26, 2013. https://www.theatlantic.com /politics/archive/2013/06/the-case-against-universal-national -service/277230/

Anna Murline Grobe, "Love of Country: US Ready for Mandatory National Service?" *The Christian Science Monitor*, June 3, 2020. https://www.csmonitor.com/USA/2020/0603/Love-of-country -US-ready-for-mandatory-national-service

Amy Rutenberg, "America Is Under Seige Due to COVID-19: Could a Year of National Service Help Us Thrive?" *National Interest*, March 25, 2020. https://nationalinterest.org/blog/buzz/america -under-siege-due-covid-19-could-year-national-service-help-us -thrive-136537

Hope Hodge Seck, "Bringing Back the Draft: 5 Possibilites for the Future of Military Conscription," Military.com, March 22, 2020. https://www.military.com/daily-news/2020/03/22/bringing-back -draft-5-possibilities-future-military-conscription.html

OPPOSING
VIEWPOINTS®
SERIES

| Should the US
| Increase or Decrease
| Military Spending?

Chapter Preface

Most Americans agree that a military is necessary to defend the nation from adversaries. The question, however, is how much of the nation's budget should be spent on defense. The issue has become particularly vexed in recent decades. The so-called war on terror has been both an excuse for increases in the defense budget and a flashpoint for criticism of waste and excess. In addition, the increased use of civilian contracts for military projects has spawned charges of corruption as well as waste.

Those who believe the US spends too much on defense argue that a nation with a broken health care system and the highest rates of infant mortality, homelessness, and food insecurity of any advanced nation cannot afford to spend money policing the rest of the world and enriching politically well-connected defense contractors.

On the other hand, those who believe the US needs to increase its military budget point out that the increasingly volatile world situation requires a strong and ever-ready military. Enemies such as terrorists and rogue nations, some with nuclear weapons, leave the US no choice but to bolster its defenses.

The authors of the viewpoints in the following chapter take a variety of approaches to this issue, and the lines between enough and too much military spending are not always clearly drawn.

In his farewell address, President Dwight D. Eisenhower warned of the dangers of a military-industrial complex, one that has only grown since his speech. You will read viewpoints arguing that Eisenhower's warning was overblown and viewpoints saying the danger is greater than ever before.

The debate about how much the US should spend defending its allies has been especially fierce lately. Here, authors take on this question, arguing on the one hand that the money is well-spent and on the other that the US should not be policeman to the world. And two of the viewpoints take a close look at the effects of the military budget on the larger economy.

> *"While there is certainly no shortage of symbiotic back-scratching between Washington and the defense industry, the notion that a shadowy cabal drives defense policy doesn't jibe with reality."*

The US Needs to Spend More on Defense, Not Less

Greg S. Jones

In recent decades, those who oppose increases in defense spending have pointed to the many non-government industries that enrich themselves through defense department contracts, often involving political corruption. In the following viewpoint, Greg S. Jones argues that while some corruption may exist, the actual percentage of the nation's income spent on defense has decreased markedly in recent years. The real danger to the nation's economy, says the author, is increases in spending on social programs, such as Medicare and programs for the poor. Greg S. Jones is a conservative commentator whose work has appeared in the Week, Reason.com, *the* Federalist, Daily Caller, *and the* American Spectator, *among others.*

"The Myth of the Military-Industrial Complex," by Greg S. Jones, *National Review*, May 4, 2017. Reprinted by permission.

As you read, consider the following questions:

1. What did President Eisenhower mean by "the military industrial complex," and why was he warning the nation about it?
2. What is the difference between discretionary spending and mandatory spending?
3. What type of spending does the author say is more of a threat to the nation than military spending?

Donald Trump's recent military overtures toward Syria and North Korea have revived one of the more resilient myths in American political history: namely, that Washington makes defense policy according to the desires of a mysterious and immensely powerful "military-industrial complex."

From former Ohio congressman Dennis Kucinich to late-night talk show host Bill Maher to former Presidential candidate Ron Paul, Trump's newfound militarism has unleashed a torrent of conspiratorial pundits bemoaning the ill-defined network of politicians, generals, and defense contractors that supposedly enriches itself at the republic's expense.

But while there is certainly no shortage of symbiotic back-scratching between Washington and the defense industry, the notion that a shadowy cabal drives defense policy doesn't jibe with reality.

The idea of a military-industrial complex originated with President Dwight D. Eisenhower, who warned in his farewell address of the increasing coziness between the state and vendors of war:

> This conjunction of an immense military establishment and a large arms industry is new in the American experience. The total influence—economic, political, and even spiritual—is felt in every State house, every office of the Federal government. We recognize the imperative for this development. Yet we must not fail to comprehend its grave implications. Our toil, resources and livelihood are all involved; so is the very structure of our society.

In the councils of government, we must guard against the acquisition of unwarranted influence, whether sought or unsought, by the military-industrial complex. The potential for the disastrous rise of misplaced power exists and will persist.

Eisenhower's words were apropos for the time. Military spending accounted for roughly 10 percent of American GDP in 1961, a staggering figure considering that the Second World War had been over for more than 15 years and the Korean War for nearly a decade. It was a time of relative peace, and yet big bucks for the defense industry.

Since then, however, defense spending has steadily declined as a proportion of GDP, albeit with a few occasional upticks; by 2016 it had shrunk to just under 3.2 percent. In fact, it has only exceeded 5 percent four times since 2001, despite America's involvement in two wars, and several war-like entanglements, over that period.

While these wars and engagements were certainly expensive in terms of real dollars, the steady decline of defense spending as a percentage of total economic output puts the lie to the idea of an all-powerful defense industry controlling the country's purse strings. And while one can certainly make the argument that the federal government spends too much money on instruments of war—and that that money is not always utilized efficiently—the military's shrinking fiscal footprint in terms of GDP should be celebrated, not disingenuously demonized.

But blind partisanship has made this particular truth inconvenient, so the leftist (and sometimes libertarian) effort to discredit the defense industry continues apace. A simple Internet image search for "defense spending meme" reveals numerous charts and diagrams purporting to show federal defense spending dominating the federal budget at the expense of nearly everything else.

These infographics are so prevalent, in fact, that left-leaning websites Politifact and FactCheck.org have stepped in to point out the obvious fallacy that plagues them: They only reference "discretionary" spending, or what Congress spends via appropriations bills, which accounts for roughly one-third of the total federal budget. "Mandatory" spending—mostly on entitlements such as Social Security, Medicare, and the SNAP food-stamp program—accounts for the lion's share of the budget. In 2015, for instance, defense spending consumed 54 percent of the discretionary spending, but only 16 percent of all federal spending.

Though I like Ike, his warning was way off the mark: the Democratic-entitlement complex is the real Leviathan threatening the integrity and spirit of America. In fact, while defense spending as a factor of GDP has steadily declined, welfare and entitlement spending has ballooned to nearly four times what it was when Ike began his second term. Social Security and Medicare alone consumed nearly three times more money than defense last year.

And that's the good news. While advances in technology, and hopefully policy, may well continue to increase the efficiency of America's defense spending, the costs of the entitlements beloved by Democrats are only set to increase. By 2047, the CBO projects that Social Security and Medicare alone will consume half of all non-interest federal spending.

Don't get me wrong: There is certainly plenty of room to streamline defense spending and reduce bureaucracy and backscratching in the Pentagon's contracting processes. But furthering belief in an all-powerful military-industrial boogeyman serves no one, particularly given the current climate.

History has demonstrated time and time again America's need for a robust, capable defense that nevertheless knows its own limits. Unfortunately, Trump has inherited a historically deficient military—a recent Heritage Foundation analysis rated America's armed forces "marginal"—and a dangerous, fast-changing geopolitical landscape. Threats abound, from Russia to China to North Korea to ISIS, and Trump has pledged to increase military spending accordingly.

But that's just good defense policy; it's not the result of some sinister conspiracy.

> *"The more the US demands host nations pay for the US presence, the less support local politicians may have to maintain the arrangement."*

America's Defense of Its Allies Is a Good Deal for the US

Michael E. Flynn, Carla Martinez Machain, and Michael A. Allen

The previous viewpoint argued that the United States needs to build back up its military budget. In the following viewpoint, Michael E. Flynn, Carla Martinez Machain, and Michael A. Allen get into the weeds regarding President Trump's demand that the nation's allies pay more for their own defense. The authors argue that the money the US government spends defending its allies is a wise investment in the nation's security and that demanding more money from allies could backfire. Michael E. Flynn and Carla Martinez Machain are associate professors of political science at Kansas State University. Michael A. Allen is associate professor of political science at Boise State University, in Boise, Idaho.

"Why Does the US Pay So Much for the Defense of Its Allies? 5 Questions Answered," Michael E. Flynn, Carla Martinez Machain, and Michael A. Allen, The Conversation Media Group Ltd, December 2, 2019. https://theconversation.com/why-does-the-us-pay -so-much-for-the-defense-of-its-allies-5-questions-answered-127683. Licensed under CC BY-ND 4.0.

As you read, consider the following questions:

1. How do stronger countries benefit from providing security for weaker countries?
2. What other expenditures do nations such as Japan and South Korea contribute to the US military beyond the payment for the military presence in their countries?
3. How do the citizens of other nations feel about the US presence there, according to the viewpoint? How do Americans feel about our support of our allies?

Since the start of Donald Trump's run for the US presidency in 2015, he has been critical of the amount of money US allies contribute to their own defense.

Now, the Trump administration is demanding that Japan and South Korea pay more for hosting US troops stationed in those countries.

The media also reported that US military leadership in South Korea discussed the possibility of withdrawing up to 4,000 troops from South Korea if it does not increase its contributions. The Pentagon has since denied having such plans.

We have each studied overseas deployments of US military personnel for nearly a decade and have recently come together to research the costs and benefits of such deployments.

What's in It for the US?

The US currently has approximately 174,000 active-duty personnel deployed to overseas locations in approximately 140 countries. The Department of Defense Comptroller's Office estimates the total cost of overseas bases and deployments at US$24.4 billion in fiscal year 2020. These figures generally exclude the costs of ongoing combat operations.

When stronger countries provide security for weaker countries, they receive non-material benefits in return.

For example, the weaker country may sacrifice control over their foreign policy and give the major power access to territory or airspace it otherwise would not have. Deployments in Japan and Korea gave the US influence in Southeast and East Asian regional matters during the Cold War.

Additionally, US military personnel have served as the forefront of US public diplomacy over the past 70 years through their routine jobs and day-to-day interactions with locals. The US has been particularly effective at building "soft power," meaning that people in other countries support the US because of the affinity they feel toward Americans and American culture.

How Long Has the US Had Bases in Japan and South Korea?

Since the end of World War II in 1945 and the Korean War in 1953, the US has maintained several military bases and tens of thousands of military personnel within both countries.

After Japan regained its sovereignty in 1951, the United States and Japan signed a treaty calling for mutual defense and an agreement that allowed for the US to operate and maintain military bases in Japan. Either country has the option, with one year's notice, to end the treaty.

Currently, there are approximately 55,000 US troops in Japan.

South Korea has hosted US forces since the Korean War, when the United Nations Security Council authorized member nations to repel North Korea's invasion of South Korea. After the 1953 armistice, the forces remained to provide continued security to South Korea and to deter hostilities from North Korea.

There are currently approximately 26,500 US troops in South Korea.

How Much Do Japan and South Korea Normally Contribute?

The United States has negotiated agreements with both Japan and South Korea that lay out the details of the cost-sharing arrangements with each country.

The specific amounts contributed, as well as the activities that each state covers, vary by country and over time. However, the contributions of US allies typically are substantial.

For example, in 2019, the US and South Korea negotiated an agreement calling for South Korea to contribute approximately $893 million.

Japan's current agreement doesn't provide a clear statement on total contributions. However, Japan's current support amounts to approximately $1.7 billion.

By comparison, the Department of Defense currently estimates the total cost of maintaining the US presence in South Korea and Japan at $4.5 billion and $5.7 billion, respectively.

Accordingly, both countries' contributions amount to a substantial percentage of these total price tags.

Importantly, these figures provide only a rough picture of the financial relationship between the host country and the US related to defense. For example, the figures for Japan do not reflect other transfers, like Japanese purchases of US weapons systems, free rent and tax waivers, and other expenditures taken on by the Japanese government.

How Do People in Other Countries View the Presence of US Military?

In 2018, we conducted a survey in 14 countries, including Japan and South Korea, with approximately 1,000 respondents in each. These countries have traditionally hosted large US military deployments.

We found that people in the host country generally feel positively or have neutral attitudes toward the US personnel stationed in their country. People who have had direct contact with members of the US military, or whose families and friends have interacted with the military, are more likely to report favorable views of US personnel.

In addition, between 10% and 25% report receiving financial benefits from the US military presence. This can include having US servicemembers patronize their businesses or being employed by the US military.

Our personal interviews with people in troop-hosting countries confirm these findings. For example, when we asked a member of the local Parish Council in the village of Lakenheath, England, how locals interact with the US military, he told us, "When they see that [US military personnel] are just as human as you are, people like [the US military] more."

Opinions are not uniform. There are certainly ethical, social, environmental and economic considerations to hosting large US deployments, and these costs have led to dissatisfaction and opposition in multiple countries.

The US presence has led to protest movements on the Japanese island of Okinawa, around the Ramstein Air Base in Germany, and in South Korea.

The more the US demands host nations pay for the US presence, the less support local politicians may have to maintain the arrangement.

Are Trump's Demands Reasonable?

The discussion of whether US allies contribute enough to their own defense is as old as many of the deployments themselves.

However, there are two components that make the Trump demands novel.

First, negotiations with South Korea previously occurred every four to five years. The Trump administration changed this last year to every year for South Korea. These negotiations are complicated and could make annual negotiations both time-consuming and turbulent.

Second, reports suggest that Trump's new demands are not based on any clear US military need. This leads us to the question of how Trump arrived at the new sum being sought from South Korea.

Polling shows that while Americans are increasingly skeptical of the US intervention into Afghanistan and Iraq, Americans do support the United States' current engagement in the world and its commitments to allies.

"There is much wisdom in increasing international engagement in diplomacy and trade while husbanding military strength."

America Should Not Be the World's Policeman

Daniel L. Davis

In the following viewpoint, Daniel L. Davis addresses, head on, the issue of what that military budget is being used for—and whether or not those uses are justified. Davis argues that the role of the US military should not be to benefit and protect US corporations. He also says that US military activities around the world have not been effective and that diplomacy would be more effective and less costly than military intervention. Daniel L. Davis is a foreign policy and defense analyst and retired lieutenant colonel in the US Army.

As you read, consider the following questions:

1. Why do you think the author says Thanassis Cambanis "does not blush," in making his case?
2. How does the author define "imperial power"?
3. How does the author envision the US military, and what does he see as the importance of economic and diplomatic engagement with the rest of the world?

"America Should Not Act as the World's Policeman," by Daniel L. Davis, the *National Interest*, January 16, 2017. Reprinted by permission.

W hy It Pays to Be the World's Policeman—Literally," written by Thanassis Cambanis in *Politico*, serves as an excellent compilation of the best neoconservative justifications for the overuse of American military power abroad. It also serves as an excellent exposé illuminating the fatal flaws of their logic. Being the world's policeman does *not* pay, and indeed, if left unchecked, could one day cost the nation dearly.

The first tactic used by those advocating the aggressive use of lethal military power abroad is to cast the matter in black-and-white, all-or-nothing terms. Cambanis tries to paint all who don't support expansionist views with the emotionally negative tag of "isolationist." The absence of a reckless policy of adventurism is hardly isolationist. Its antithesis is intelligent restraint.

There is much wisdom in increasing international engagement in diplomacy and trade while husbanding military strength. Such a philosophy increases global engagement, increases business opportunity for American goods, and ensures that the military instrument will be sharp and ready to defend the country if necessary. That is as far from "isolationist" as one can get. Unfortunately, the word that comes closest to accurately describing the worldview advocated by some neocons is "imperial."

The definition of imperial is "characterizing the rule or authority of a sovereign state over its dependencies; domineering, imperious." Cambanis doesn't hesitate—or blush—in listing the benefits to maintaining an aggressive military-based foreign policy. He writes:

> America runs a world order that might have some collateral benefits for other countries, but is largely built around US interests: to enrich America and American business; to keep Americans safe while creating jobs and profits for America's military-industrial complex; and to make sure that America retains, as long as possible, its position as the richest, dominant global superpower. … America's steering role in numerous regions—NATO, Latin America, and the Arabian peninsula— gives it leverage to call the shots on matters of great important to American security and the bottom line. … America's "global

cop" role means that shipping lanes, free trade agreements, oil exploration deals, ad hoc military coalitions, and so on are maintained to the benefit of the US government or US corporations.

To say the United States "runs" the world order, to boast that massive defense spending is a good "jobs program" and that a key function of the US Navy is not the defense of the nation but to give "US corporations" financial security, is the very definition of an imperial power. I find such ideas obscene. More importantly, however, these views are dangerously flawed and overlook some critical facts.

First, those who support expansionist views fail to recognize that such imperial behaviors engender the hatred of many in the world—just as it engendered hatred of the British crown by our forefathers two centuries ago. This is not a minor problem. Anti-Americanism fuels the ambitions of those who would wish our country harm and increases the chances they'll act against our interests. From Al Qaeda to ISIS to Russia and the leaders of other groups and governments, favorability ratings for the United States are dangerously low in key areas of the world.

Second, the implication that the use of the military in scores of countries around the world has helped the United States is flatly and demonstrably wrong. Over the past decade, the United States has fought or is currently fighting in Iraq, Afghanistan, Syria, Libya, Somalia, Africa and covertly in many other locations. The security environment in none of these locations has been improved as a result. To the contrary, the threat to American interests is higher in every single location than it was prior to the deployment of military power. That is clearly not the way to buttress American national security and economic prosperity.

Third, advocates of the imperial worldview incorrectly posit that the only way to "enrich" the United States is to dominate the rest of the globe militarily. Such thinking is an insult to the citizens of this country. Quite to the contrary, the American worker is industrious, intelligent, creative and driven to succeed. Instead of predicating our financial security on sending the armed forces to military dominate and "call the shots" abroad, we would benefit far more by increasing our international engagement by focusing on expanding commercial markets, expanding win-win trade relations and increasing the use of diplomacy.

As a retired Army officer, I am a strong advocate of maintaining a strong military. I am not at all suggesting gutting defense. To the contrary, I advocate a reformation of the armed forces that will result in a more powerful military that won't bankrupt the nation. But the power of this dominant military should be maintained at a high state of readiness and not perpetually dissipated by overuse abroad. Its strength and readiness should be preserved to guarantee the security of the country.

Increasing economic and diplomatic engagement with the world, reducing the knee-jerk application of lethal military power abroad, and preserving the power of the Armed Forces to guarantee national security are the best means of ensuring a strong America. Such a restrained foreign policy will raise America's influence abroad, improve the domestic economy and strengthen our national security.

> *"This new coalition of companies, agencies, and lobbyists dwarfs the system known by Eisenhower when he warned Americans to 'guard against the acquisition of unwarranted influence... by the military-industrial complex.'"*

The Economy Has Become Dependent on War, Making Opposition Useless

Jonathan Turley

Previous viewpoints have discussed the military industrial complex and its role in the defense budget. In the following viewpoint, Jonathan Turley describes what he calls "the new military-industrial complex" and argues that it is even bigger and more dangerous than the one Eisenhower warned against, siphoning money from worthier needs and keeping the country in a perpetual war that costs not only money, but lives. Jonathan Turley is the Shapiro Professor of Public Interest Law at George Washington University and has testified before Congress on the dangerous expansion of presidential powers.

"Big Money Behind War: The Military-Industrial Complex," by Jonathan Turley, Al Jazeera Media Network, January 11, 2014. Reprinted by permission.

As you read, consider the following questions:

1. What does the author say is the "ambiguous enemy" that justifies and supports the new military-industrial complex?
2. Who stands to gain from a perpetual war?
3. How are environmental and social programs harmed by the military-industrial complex described in the viewpoint?

I n January 1961, US President Dwight D. Eisenhower used his farewell address to warn the nation of what he viewed as one of its greatest threats: the military-industrial complex composed of military contractors and lobbyists perpetuating war.

Eisenhower warned that "an immense military establishment and a large arms industry" had emerged as a hidden force in US politics and that Americans "must not fail to comprehend its grave implications." The speech may have been Eisenhower's most courageous and prophetic moment. Fifty years and some later, Americans find themselves in what seems like perpetual war. No sooner do we draw down on operations in Iraq than leaders demand an intervention in Libya or Syria or Iran. While perpetual war constitutes perpetual losses for families, and ever expanding budgets, it also represents perpetual profits for a new and larger complex of business and government interests.

The new military-industrial complex is fuelled by a conveniently ambiguous and unseen enemy: the terrorist. Former President George W Bush and his aides insisted on calling counter-terrorism efforts a "war." This concerted effort by leaders like former Vice President Dick Cheney (himself the former CEO of defence-contractor Halliburton) was not some empty rhetorical exercise. Not only would a war maximise the inherent powers of the president, but it would maximise the budgets for military and homeland agencies.

This new coalition of companies, agencies, and lobbyists dwarfs the system known by Eisenhower when he warned Americans to "guard against the acquisition of unwarranted influence... by the military-industrial complex." Ironically, it has had some of its best days under President Barack Obama who has radically expanded drone attacks and claimed that he alone determines what a war is for the purposes of consulting Congress.

Good for Economy?

While few politicians are willing to admit it, we don't just endure wars we seem to need war—at least for some people. A study showed that roughly 75 percent of the fallen in these wars come from working class families. They do not need war. They pay the cost of the war. Eisenhower would likely be appalled by the size of the industrial and governmental workforce committed to war or counter-terrorism activities. Military and homeland budgets now support millions of people in an otherwise declining economy. Hundreds of billions of dollars flow each year from the public coffers to agencies and contractors who have an incentive to keep the country on a war-footing—and footing the bill for war.

Across the country, the war-based economy can be seen in an industry which includes everything from Homeland Security educational degrees to counter-terrorism consultants to private-run preferred traveller programmes for airport security gates. Recently, the "black budget" of secret intelligence programmes alone was estimated at $52.6bn for 2013. That is only the secret programmes, not the much larger intelligence and counterintelligence budgets. We now have 16 spy agencies that employ 107,035 employees. This is separate from the over one million people employed by the military and national security law enforcement agencies.

The core of this expanding complex is an axis of influence of corporations, lobbyists, and agencies that have created a massive, self-sustaining terror-based industry.

The Contractors

In the last eight years, trillions of dollars have flowed to military and homeland security companies. When the administration starts a war like Libya, it is a windfall for companies who are given generous contracts to produce everything from replacement missiles to ready-to-eat meals.

In the first 10 days of the Libyan war alone, the administration spent roughly $550m. That figure includes about $340m for munitions—mostly cruise missiles that must be replaced. Not only did Democratic members of Congress offer post-hoc support for the Libyan attack, but they also proposed a permanent authorisation for presidents to attack targets deemed connected to terrorism—a perpetual war on terror. The Department of Homeland Security (DHS) offers an even steadier profit margin. According to Morgan Keegan, a wealth management and capital firm, investment in homeland security companies is expected to yield a 12 percent annual growth through 2013—an astronomical return when compared to other parts of the tanking economy.

The Lobbyists

There are thousands of lobbyists in Washington to guarantee the ever-expanding budgets for war and homeland security. One such example is former DHS Secretary Michael Chertoff who pushed the purchase of the heavily criticised (and little tested) full-body scanners used in airports. When Chertoff was giving dozens of interviews to convince the public that the machines were needed to hold back the terror threat, many people were unaware that the manufacturer of the machine is a client of the Chertoff Group, his highly profitable security consulting agency. (Those hugely expensive machines were later scrapped after Rapiscan, the manufacturer, received the windfall.)

Lobbyists maintain pressure on politicians by framing every budget in "tough on terror" versus "soft on terror" terms. They have the perfect products to pitch—products that are designed to destroy themselves and be replaced in an ever-lasting war on terror.

The Agencies

It is not just revolving doors that tie federal agencies to these lobbyists and companies. The war-based economy allows for military and homeland departments to be virtually untouchable. Environmental and social programmes are eliminated or curtailed by billions as war-related budgets continue to expand to meet "new threats."

With the support of an army of lobbyists and companies, cabinet members like former DHS Secretary Janet Napolitano, are invincible in Washington. When citizens complained of watching their children groped by the TSA, Napolitano defiantly retorted that if people did not want their children groped, they should yield and use the unpopular full-body machines—the machines being sold by her predecessor, Chertoff.

It is not just the Defense and DHS departments that enjoy the war windfall. Take the Department of Justice (DOJ). A massive counterterrorism system has been created employing tens of thousands of personnel with billions of dollars to search for domestic terrorists. The problem has been a comparative shortage of actual terrorists to justify the size of this internal security system.

Accordingly, the DOJ has counted everything from simple immigration cases to credit card fraud as terror cases in a body count approach not seen since the Vietnam War. For example, the DOJ claimed to have busted a major terror-network as part of "Operation Cedar Sweep," where Lebanese citizens were accused of sending money to terrorists. They were later forced to drop all charges against all 27 defendants as unsupportable. It turned out to be a bunch of simple head shops. Nevertheless, the new internal security system continues to grind on with expanding powers and budgets. A few years ago, the DOJ even changed the definition of terrorism to allow for an ever-widening number of cases to be considered "terror-related."

Symbiotic Relationship

Our economic war-dependence is matched by political war-dependence. Many members represent districts with contractors that supply homeland security needs and our on-going wars.

Even with polls showing that the majority of Americans are opposed to continuing the wars in Iraq and Afghanistan, the new military-industrial complex continues to easily muster the necessary support from both Democrats and Republicans in Congress. It is a testament to the influence of this alliance that hundreds of billions are being spent in Afghanistan and Iraq while Congress is planning to cut billions from core social programmes, including a possible rollback on Medicare due to lack of money. None of that matters. It doesn't even matter that Afghan President Hamid Karzai has called the US the enemy and said he wishes that he had joined the Taliban. Even the documented billions stolen by government officials in Iraq and Afghanistan are treated as a mere cost of doing business. It is what Eisenhower described as the "misplaced power" of the military-industrial complex—power that makes public opposition and even thousands of dead soldiers immaterial. War may be hell for some but it is heaven for others in a war-dependent economy.

> *"Accommodating the smaller amount of funding under this option would require DoD to decrease the size of its forces, slow the rate at which it modernizes weapon systems, or do both."*

Reduce the Department of Defense Budget

Congressional Budget Office

In other viewpoints in this chapter, the authors have discussed the various reasons for increasing or limiting the military budget. In the following viewpoint, the US Congressional Budget Office (CBO) finds that in addition to effects on the budget, decreasing appropriations for defense would not only force the military to reduce personnel, but to cut back on innovative new weapons systems. Nonetheless, states the author, the US would remain, by far, the world's largest military. The Congressional Budget Office is a non-partisan agency within the legislative branch of the government that provides information to Congress to aid them in making legislative decisions.

"Reduce the Department of Defense's Budget," Congressional Budget Office, December 13, 2018.

As you read, consider the following questions:

1. Why does the military need more sophisticated weaponry, according to this report?
2. What is one argument the CBO cites for *not* reducing the defense budget?
3. How does the CBO suggest that any potential cuts should be made?

The Department of Defense (DoD) received $616 billion in appropriations for its base budget in 2019, the highest amount since 2010 (after adjusting for inflation). The Department's Future Years Defense Plan (FYDP) for 2019 anticipates that base-budget levels will average about $650 billion per year (in 2019 dollars) through 2023. (DoD's base budget is intended to fund enduring activities, such as day-to-day military and civilian operations and development and procurement of weapon systems. It does not include additional funding appropriated for nonpermanent activities, such as overseas contingency operations or other emergencies.) Before 2019, the amount appropriated in 2010 had been the highest for DoD's base budget, which had grown by 50 percent since 2000, and surpassed even the 1985 budget, DoD's largest peacetime budget during the Cold War. After 2012, DoD's base budgets decreased under the constraints of the Budget Control Act of 2011 (BCA), averaging about $550 billion for 2013 through 2018.

Option

This option encompasses two alternative decreases in DoD's budget. The first would reduce DoD's budget over three years so that funding in 2022 would be 10 percent less than the funding planned for that year in the Administration's 2019 FYDP. The second would reduce DoD's budget by 5 percent over that same period. Both alternatives would allow for real (inflation-adjusted) growth of 1 percent annually after 2022.

THE COSTS AND BENEFITS OF INCREASED MILITARY SPENDING

The United States spends the most money of any country on military budgets at $598.5 billion dollars annually, which accounts for over 54% of all federal spending. Trump plans to take government spending from a variety of programs ranging from the departments of health, education, and environment to pay for the increase in military spending.

Through this expansion of military spending the White House calls for a 24% cut to the EPA's budget, according to the Trump administration. Such a move would have a huge impact on environmental health, which affects the health of our citizens. Through the EPA, a variety of steps are taken to ensure public safety, including the protection of lands, species, and water quality for citizens to drink.

The EPA would not be the only program affected. According to the *New York Times*, other agencies that would be affected by this plan would be the I.R.S, where budgets would be slashed by 14%. With these cuts to the I.R.S. budget, the amount of investigations towards tax fraud, money laundering, identity theft, and cyber crime would decrease.

Though there is an opposition to more military spending, many … people feel as though the increase in military spending will increase our safety. Groups such as ISIS provoke fear throughout our country, leading to the belief that with a larger military budget we will be able to increase our technology, training, and border control workforce, enabling our borders and citizens to be protected.

This increase in spending may provide other benefits as well. According to former Secretary of Labor Robert Reich, the military provides over 3.5 million individuals with jobs. Without these jobs our unemployment rate would go from 9.5% to over 11.5%. Therefore, more military spending will decrease the unemployment rate and provide more citizens with work.

Though these benefits are helpful, where is the line drawn between too much military spending when these funds could be implemented elsewhere? This is something for the citizens to speak up and decide upon together to create a better country for us to live in.

"The Costs and Benefits of Increased Military Spending," The Bottom Line, March 7, 2017.

Effects on the Budget

Under the first alternative, funding for DoD in 2022 would be $637 billion, excluding funding for overseas contingency operations. That amount would still be large by historical standards; adjusted for inflation, it would be roughly in line with DoD's base budget in 2012, the last budget prepared before the BCA's caps were applied, and more than Cold War spending at its height. Through 2028, cumulative funding for DoD would be reduced by $591 billion under the first alternative. That estimate of savings is based on the costs of plans outlined in the 2019 FYDP (which defines plans and costs through 2023) and the Congressional Budget Office's projections of costs over the following five years. Under the second alternative, savings would total $284 billion through 2028.

Savings would be smaller if DoD needed more than three years to implement the reductions under this option or if the costs of current plans were overstated. Conversely, savings could be larger if costs to implement current plans were underestimated. For example, DoD has frequently underestimated its costs to develop and purchase weapon systems.

Other Effects

Accommodating the smaller amount of funding under this option would require DoD to decrease the size of its forces, slow the rate at which it modernizes weapon systems, or do both. Force cuts could be made proportionally across the services or could be tailored to the specific needs of parts of the military. Similarly, to achieve a desired pace of modernization, DoD would need to balance the goal of maintaining a particular force size against the goal of procuring new weapons. (CBO's estimate of savings in outlays is based on proportional reductions to each part of DoD's budget.)

With a somewhat smaller force, DoD's ability to execute all the elements in the current national security strategy would be lessened. The current strategy envisions prevailing at both the low end of the spectrum of conflict (for example, counterinsurgency operations) and at the high end (conflicts with Russia or China). Simultaneously pursuing those goals is expensive. For example, at the same time that the Army has soldiers in more than 140 countries, all four military services are buying highly sophisticated military weaponry to fight against Russia or China, and DoD is modernizing all elements of its nuclear forces. Under this option, DoD would need to focus its efforts on the most important elements of national security, cut back in some other areas, and rely more on both conventional and nuclear deterrence to dissuade Russia and China from attacks on the United States, its interests, or its allies. For instance, DoD might need to scale back or eliminate the Army's presence in some countries and replace that military effort with other instruments of national power. Such a shift from military to nonmilitary engagement would not be inconsistent with the Summary of the 2018 National Defense Strategy of the United States of America, which calls for "the seamless integration of multiple elements of national power—diplomacy, information, economics, finance, intelligence, law enforcement, and military." The reduced size of the military and concurrent shift to a more integrated approach would require greater patience in addressing crises around the world, however: Diplomacy rarely offers the dramatic action (or speed) of military intervention.

One argument against this option is that the size and number of military operations that could be conducted simultaneously and the duration for which they could be sustained would be diminished. Under Army policy, for example, three active brigade combat teams (BCTs) are required to support the rotation of a single BCT in and out of a combat zone. Consequently, the number of BCTs that the Army could continuously deploy would decrease by one for every three active BCTs that were cut from the force structure. Similar considerations would apply to the deployment of naval and air forces. If the need for a large, sustained military presence overseas arose, DoD could increase the size of its forces at that time (as it has done often in the past), but it could take a few years.

Despite the reduced military capacity under this option, the United States would remain the world's preeminent military power. Even in 2022, when funding would be lowest under this option in both nominal and inflation-adjusted terms, it would be nearly double the combined military spending of China and Russia in 2017.

> *"The real issue is what is an 'adequate' amount of military spending, given that every extra dollar spent above the necessary level is a clear loss for the economy as a whole."*

Excessive Military Spending Sucks Money from the Rest of the Economy

Andrew Beattie

Other authors in this chapter have touched on the effects of the military budget on the overall economy. In the following viewpoint, Andrew Beattie takes a closer look at that aspect of military spending, discussing the trade-offs of maintaining a large military and how that decision is made by democratic nations versus non-democratic ones. Andrew Beattie is a journalist who covers finance.

As you read, consider the following questions:

1. Why is military spending less of a drag on the United States than it is on some other nations?
2. How does the military siphon jobs from the private sector?
3. What does the author mean by "the guns and butter curve"?

"How Military Spending Affects the Economy," by Andrew Beattie, Dotdash, September 29, 2018. Reprinted by permission.

T he Stockholm International Peace Research Institute (SIPRI) has excellent data on military spending by nation. According to SIPRI research, the five biggest spenders in 2018 were the United States, China, Saudi Arabia, India, and France. Together, these countries made up around 60% of global military spending. In 2018, US military expenditure increased by almost 4.6% to $633.5 Billion. China increased its military spending by 5%, Saudi Arabia decreased its spending by 6.5% and India increased its military spending by 3.1%.[1] As with any government spending, these dollars have an impact.

The Why of Military Spending

Military spending is one area where there is no private solution to replace the public purse. No single corporation or group of citizens is sufficiently motivated (or trustworthy) enough to take financial responsibility for the cost of having a military. Adam Smith, one of the fathers of free market economics, identified the defense of society as one of the primary functions of government and justification for reasonable taxation.[2, 3] Basically, the government is acting on behalf of the public to ensure that the military is sufficiently well resourced to defend the nation. In practice, however, defending the nation expands to defending a nation's strategic interests, and the whole concept of "sufficient" is up for debate as other nations also bulk up their militaries.

The Hole That Debt Built

Capital is finite, and capital going into one spending category means that there is less money for something else. This fact gets more interesting when we consider that any government spending exceeding revenues results in a deficit that is added to the national debt. The ballooning national debt has an economic impact on everyone, and military spending is one of many contributing factors.[4] As the national debt grows, the interest expense of the debt grows and the cost of borrowing subtly increases due to the risk that increased debt represents. In theory, the increased debt will also drag on economic growth and eventually a driver towards higher taxes.

As of now, however, the US, in particular, has enjoyed generous debt terms from domestic and international lenders, so the role that military spending plays in increasing the debt is generally not focused on.[5, 6] Some advocates for decreased military spending might tie it to a certain percentage increase in the mortgage rates people pay, given the relationship between treasury yields and commercial lending.[7] This reasoning holds and military spending does sit as a large percentage of discretionary spending.[8]

In other nations, particularly ones that are still developing economically, a focus on military spending often means foregoing other important spending priorities. There are many nations that have a standing military but an unreliable public infrastructure, from hospitals to roads to schools.[9, 10, 11] North Korea is an extreme example of what an unrelenting focus on military spending can do to the standard of living for the general population.[12, 13] The generous debt terms that the US enjoys are far from universal, so the trade-off between military spending and public infrastructure is more painful for many nations.[5]

Employment

Jobs are a big part of the economic impact of military spending. Of course, there are the active troops, but there is also a considerable infrastructure built up around them that requires contractors, trades, consultants, and so on to support the military. Then there are the private businesses that spring up as a result of the military spending, including everything from weapons manufacturers to the restaurants that pop up near military bases.[14] Here again, a free market economist would point out that the public dollars going to support those jobs directly or indirectly are actually sucking the equivalent number of jobs—or more—out of the private economy due to the taxation needed to create them.

It really comes down to whether or not you believe a standing military is a necessity. If it is, then some jobs will need to be sacrificed in the private sector to make that happen. Of course, people will still argue about what size a standing military should be. That's as much a political question as an economic one.

Technological Developments

Another argument for the negative economic impact of military spending is that there is a diversion of talent and technical skills towards supporting military research and development. This appears to be a bit unfair as, in the past, military research has benefited the private economy as technological leaps and talented people flowed back and forth. Military research has been vital to the creation of microwaves, the Internet, GPS, etc.[15, 16, 17] In fact, part of the reason we have drones taking wedding photos and potentially delivering packages for Amazon is that much of the expense of creating the basic technology was covered through military spending.[18]

There are definitely some distorting factors that military R&D has on research and technology, but the research spending isn't an entire loss for the economy as many of the breakthroughs do positively influence commercial technology.

Guns and Butter

The guns and butter curve is a classic illustration of how there is an opportunity cost to every expenditure. If you believe a standing military is a necessity for a nation, then the size of that military can be argued about but the existence of a military cannot. There is an economic cost to having defense spending that shows up in the national debt and in a dislocation of potential jobs from the private sector to the public. There is also an economic distortion of any industry that the military relies on as resources are diverted to produce better fighter planes, drones, and guns. All of these costs are necessary for a nation to bear if they are to defend themselves. We give up some butter to have guns.

The Bottom Line

The real issue is what is an "adequate" amount of military spending, given that every extra dollar spent above the necessary level is a clear loss for the economy as a whole.[4] In a democracy, that issue is debated by publicly elected officials and changes year to year. For example, military spending in the US has been declining as military engagements abroad wrap up.[19] In non-democratic nations, however, the level of adequate spending is decided by a select few and may come at even a greater cost to the country's citizens.

Endnotes

1. The Stockholm International Peace Research Institute. "Data for all countries from 1988–2018 in constant (2017) USD," Pages 15–21. Accessed April 23, 2020.
2. The Library of Economics and Liberty. "An Inquiry into the Nature and Causes of the Wealth of Nations—Book V, Chapter l." Accessed April 23, 2020.
3. The Library of Economics and Liberty. "An Inquiry into the Nature and Causes of the Wealth of Nations—Book IV, Chapter 5." Accessed April 23, 2020.
4. Committee for a Responsible Federal Budget. "CBO: Consequences of a Growing National Debt." Accessed April 23, 2020.
5. TreasuryDirect. "Summary Schedules of Federal Debt—Daily, Unaudited." Accessed April 23, 2020.
6. US Government Accountability Office. "Action Is Needed to Address the Federal Government's Fiscal Future—Highlights." Accessed April 23, 2020.
7. US Department of the Treasury. "Interest Rates—Frequently Asked Questions." Accessed April 23, 2020.
8. National Priorities Project. "Federal Spending: Where Does the Money Go." Accessed April 23, 2020.
9. Ipsos. "Global Infrastructure Index 2019," Pages 8–9. Accessed April 23, 2020.
10. The Social Progress Imperative. "Global | View the Index." Accessed April 23, 2020.
11. The World Bank. "Military Expenditure (% of GDP)." Accessed April 23, 2020.
12. Liberty in North Korea. "The People's Challenges." Accessed April 23, 2020.
13. Council on Foreign Relations. "North Korea's Military Capabilities." Accessed April 23, 2020.
14. Congressional Research Service. "Defense Primer: Department of Defense Contractors." Accessed April 23, 2020.
15. NASA. "Global Positioning System History." Accessed April 23, 2020.
16. National Science Foundation. "A Brief History of NSF and the Internet." Accessed April 18, 2020.
17. Institute of Electrical and Electronics Engineers. "A Brief History of the Microwave Oven." Accessed April 23, 2020.
18. Army University Press. "Unmanned Aerial Systems: A Historical Perspective," Pages 127–131. Accessed April 23, 2020.
19. The World Bank. "Military expenditure (% of general government expenditure)—United States." Accessed April 23, 2020.

Periodical and Internet Sources Bibliography

The following articles have been selected to supplement the diverse views presented in this chapter.

Sarah Almukhtar and Rod Nordland, "What Did the US Get for $2 Trillion in Afghanistan?" *New York Times*, December 9, 2019. https://www.nytimes.com/interactive/2019/12/09/world/middleeast/afghanistan-war-cost.html

Elisabeth Braw, "Stop Worrying and Learn to Love the Military-Industrial Complex," *Wall Street Journal*, January 2, 2019. https://www.wsj.com/articles/stop-worrying-and-learn-to-love-the-military-industrial-complex-11546473315

William J. Burns, "The United States Needs a New Foreign Policy," *Atlantic*, July 14, 2020. https://www.theatlantic.com/ideas/archive/2020/07/united-states-needs-new-foreign-policy/614110/

Alex Horton and Aaron Gregg, "Use of Military Contractors Shrouds the True Cost of War. Washington Wants It That Way, Study Says," *Washington Post*, June 30, 2020. https://www.washingtonpost.com/national-security/2020/06/30/military-contractor-study/

Michael Moran, "What Trump Gets Right About Alliances," *Foreign Policy*, December 5, 2019. https://foreignpolicy.com/2019/12/05/trump-right-alliances-free-riding-american-military-might-nato-japan-south-korea/

Michael E. O'Hanlon, "Why We Need a More Modern and Ready Military, Not a Larger One," Brookings, October 4, 2019. https://www.brookings.edu/blog/order-from-chaos/2019/10/04/why-we-need-a-more-modern-and-ready-military-not-a-larger-one/

Matt Taibbi, "The Pentagon's Bottomless Money Pit," *Rolling Stone*, March 17, 2019. https://www.rollingstone.com/politics/politics-features/pentagon-budget-mystery-807276/

Mark Thompson, "Adding Up the Cost of Our Never-Ending Wars," Pogo.org, December 17, 2019. https://www.pogo.org/analysis/2019/12/adding-up-the-cost-of-our-never-ending-wars/

OPPOSING
VIEWPOINTS®
SERIES

CHAPTER 3

Who Should Be Allowed to Serve?

Chapter Preface

In chapter 1 of this volume, the authors were concerned with whether or not citizens should be compelled to serve in the United States military. In this chapter, the debate is about who should be *allowed* to serve. As women and LGBTQ Americans have gained more rights, they have also demanded the right to serve in the military.

After reading chapter 1, you might expect that the military would welcome anyone who is both willing and able to help defend the nation. However, that is not the case. Women and LGBTQ individuals have struggled to be accepted in the military. Until quite recently, women were not allowed to serve in combat positions and LGBTQ Americans could not serve openly. These policies have changed, but the controversy is still very much alive.

Challenges to allowing women in combat and LGBTQ people in the military at all are based on a variety of objections and concerns. When it comes to women serving, critics say that women are not physically or emotionally capable of serving in combat, that the presence of women would be bad for morale, or that the risk of sexual abuse or sexual relationships between service members would be too high.

Objections to LGBTQ service members can focus on some of the same arguments regarding sexual relationships but often center on the cost to the military of providing health care to transgender service members.

The following viewpoints examine a variety of these objections. You will hear from current and former members of the military as well as journalists. In addition, a few of these authors give a bit of the history of the US military's policies regarding who is and who is not allowed to serve and under what conditions.

| "The US military's combat arms branches do not need to ban women. They need to fix their standards problem."

Women Should Be Allowed to Serve in Combat if They Can Meet the Standards

Micah Ables

In the following viewpoint, Micah Ables argues that women should be allowed to serve in combat if they can meet the same requirements male soldiers are expected to meet. He presents his argument by addressing the issues brought up by an article that appeared in the Wall Street Journal. *He doesn't disagree with all of the points made by that author but offers different solutions. Micah Ables is commander of one of the army's first mixed-gender mechanized infantry companies. He is a graduate of Ranger, Airborne, and Air Assault schools.*

"Women Aren't the Problem. Standards Are," by Micah Ables, Modern War Institute, February 5, 2019. Reprinted by permission.

As you read, consider the following questions:

1. Why, according to the viewpoint, is it wrongheaded to consider averages when determining if women should be allowed to serve in combat?
2. How does the author use his own story to make his point?
3. What sort of different skills and perspectives does the author say women bring to the military?

C hanging culture takes time.

It took the US infantry fifty-five years and thousands of deaths to abandon the idea of trench warfare. It took the US cavalry twenty-five years to accept that armored tanks were better than horses against a machine gun. It took the US Supreme Court almost sixty years to decide that "separate but equal" was anything but equal and black Americans should attend school alongside white ones. It took America more than 130 years to declare that men and women should have equal voting rights. Just because policies take time and adjustments to "get it right" does not mean that they should be abandoned altogether. Women serving in combat roles is no exception: implementation and standards should be addressed, but the policy aim is right.

Last month, Heather Mac Donald's *Wall Street Journal* op-ed argued that "women don't belong in combat units." In it, Mac Donald makes four main claims: first, that women are physiologically incapable of handling combat; second, that women cannot meet physical standards; next, that the "inevitable introduction of eros" will erode unit cohesion; and, finally, that military policies should only be made to improve combat effectiveness. While I agree with many of her premises and beliefs, I disagree with her conclusion. The US military's combat arms branches do not need to ban women. They need to fix their standards problem.

Stress and Injuries

Mac Donald is correct in asserting that men's and women's bodies are different. We are physiologically different and, on average, a man's body can handle more weight and physical hardship than a woman's. But an average is no reason to categorically ban a population. Most average Americans cannot meet the basic eligibility standards to join the military; applying Mac Donald's logic to that fact and ceasing to allow any Americans into the armed services more clearly demonstrates her logic's absurdity. That's why standards are applied individually; if an individual can meet the qualifying standard, he or she should be permitted to do the job.

I am slimmer and slighter than most of my infantry peers, a problem many female infantry aspirants also face. Upon commissioning, I weighed 155 pounds; I soon tore my shoulder labrum while grappling in training with soldiers thirty to seventy pounds heavier. I didn't have time for surgery, so I carried on and went to Infantry Basic Officer Leader Course, where I gritted my teeth through a collapsed arch in my foot. Pressing forward, I went to Ranger School, which I flunked after contracting pneumonia. As soon as I was medically cleared to start walking, I ran to Airborne School before eventually returning to complete Ranger School. Years later, I assumed company command with Achilles tendinitis and a partially torn bicep, but I did not let that stop me from leading my company on runs, on ruck marches, and in combat training.

Physical injuries are part of the job, part of pushing and trying to meet a standard. One of the Army sayings I hate most is, "You gotta break a few eggs to make an omelet." But it rings true in the sense that combat (and training for combat) produces injuries. Some people, regardless of gender, handle the strain of combat and training better than others.

And yes, as she points out, medical bills for combat-battered bodies are expensive. God forbid she ever sees the medical bills for my platoon sergeant, who nearly lost both his legs in an IED blast, or those of double-amputee Capt. Nick Vogt, or the cost of treating Lance Corp. Kyle Carpenter's shattered arm, face, and brain. For all those willing to lay down their lives and batter their bodies in combat to support and defend the Constitution of the United States against all enemies, foreign and domestic, we should be grateful to pay those bills.

Physical Standards

Once again, I agree with Mac Donald's argument that physical standards should be the same across the board. We are not alone in that sentiment. But, again, this is a standards problem—not a women-in-combat-arms problem.

Though I agree with Mac Donald's premise—that physical standards should be the same across the board—there is a problem with her argument. "Gender neutral" requirements are actually the gold standard in combat-focused training, not a punchline to be mocked. What gender-neutral Army standards exist were not created to qualify more women, as Mac Donald claims; they were designed to ensure that standards were not lowered just to qualify more women. Ranger School, for instance, is one of the few places in the Army that has always had single, and thus gender-neutral, standards—because there, the standards are tied to combat tasks, not arbitrary age- or gender-based goals.

Mac Donald points out that only two out of thirty-six women have passed Marine infantry officer training. Similarly, only three out of the first nineteen women to attempt Ranger School passed. To me, this demonstrates that gender-neutral standards work. If Mac Donald's sky-is-falling claims were true, thirty-six Marine females and nineteen female Rangers would have passed due to diluted standards. Instead, the opposite is true. At times, male Navy SEAL candidates have faced 20-percent pass rates at their initial training; it is not unusual for more than half of an all-male Ranger School class to fail the initial physical fitness assessment, and some classes have seen pass rates drop as low as 35 percent; all-male Army Special Forces training consistently hovers around a 30-percent pass rate. We don't ban men from those programs because of their low pass rates; we point to them as evidence that the standards work to separate qualified men from unqualified ones.

Where Mac Donald does have a valid point is that female combat recruits should have to "meet the same physical standards as men." But I propose changing that statement to read: "all combat soldiers should have to meet the same physical standards." My—and many others'—frustration with the current physical fitness standards is the arbitrary nature of age- or gender-specific scales. Under current fitness standards based on age and gender, my thirty-seven-year-old former platoon sergeant must run two miles in 18:18 to pass with the minimum sixty points. But if one of our twenty-year-old privates were to take that long, he would score only twenty-seven points and fail. Yet we were all expected to carry the same weapons, perform the same tasks, and go on the same patrols in Afghanistan. And yes, the current physical fitness standards for women are even more skewed than for old men.

The current standards for anyone to enter combat arms are not sufficient. I once had a male soldier, fresh out of all-male infantry basic training, fall out of a ruck march after less than a quarter mile with only thirty-five pounds of weight on his back—thirty-five pounds which the Platoon then had to carry for the next eight miles. I also led a company ruck march where two male soldiers fainted and one male noncommissioned officer outright quit, while one female soldier refused to stop walking even as she wheezed through an asthma attack. While serving in the Army's only air assault division, I had a young male soldier repeatedly fail to meet the basic gender-neutral physical standards required to attend Air Assault School. These soldiers' genders did not help or hurt our unit; their fitness, fortitude, and abilities—or lack thereof—did. The solution to these problems is to create appropriate, realistic, age- and gender-neutral standards for combat arms—not to ban any entire demographic group because there is a weak standard in place.

Hormones and Eros and Sex, Oh My!

I appreciate Mac Donald not reiterating my favorite line of ridiculous argument—that male soldiers can't stop themselves from sexually assaulting female soldiers. But this "hormonally charged" argument isn't much better.

I particularly enjoy Mac Donald's pearl clutching over male Marines doing a handstand around females. Oh the horror! I can only imagine how much Mac Donald would have blushed had she seen my all-male squad's frolicking "dance off"—with handstands galore—in the barracks after a tough, muddy, stressful week of infantry training.

But seriously, will there be inappropriate fraternization like sexual liaisons, rivalries, and breakups that undermine team bonding? Undoubtedly. I took over my current company as it was recovering from the aftershock of a consensual, male/female, NCO/soldier sexual relationship. It was handled according to Army Regulations and the Uniform Code of Military Justice—the standard—and the company moved on, learning and rebuilding trust as we went.

As some of Mac Donald's points illustrate, there is also a disturbing power imbalance present in most sexual liaisons that make consent difficult to determine. I was serving as a young platoon leader at Fort Campbell when accusations arose of a male squad leader who was repeatedly using his rank to coerce numerous subordinate soldiers into sexual liaisons in his all-male unit during a combat deployment. The fallout stemming from that situation certainly harmed their fighting force. This is nothing new; problems arising from power imbalances, sexual liaisons, rivalries, and breakups have been present in militaries for millennia—long before women joined the combat arms.

As a commander, my concern with fraternization is not solely about sex; that issue is just one part of a larger problem across the Army. During my time in command, I've also been surprised and concerned to find young team leaders on a first-name basis with their senior platoon sergeants. It's almost a weekly battle of whack-a-mole to chase down stories of squad leaders and NCOs throwing weekend parties for their favorite junior soldiers. What some call bonding and "guy stuff," the Army prohibits in Army Regulation 600-20 as "undue familiarity." A junior soldier who spends time hanging out with, drinking with, and doing God-knows-what with a senior NCO with whom he is on a first-name basis is every bit as damaging as a sexual liaison to building esprit de corps in a unified fighting force. Once again, the problem isn't women; it's failing to meet the standard.

I absolutely expect my male soldiers not to sexually assault or have inappropriate relations with female soldiers; that doesn't mean we should ban female soldiers from combat units. I also expect my soldiers not to beat their spouses or drive drunk; does that mean we should ban marriage or driving in combat units? Of course not. It just means we need to do a better job enforcing standards and discipline.

Policy Aims

Once again, I concur—this time without qualification—with Mac Donald's argument about the aims of military policies. Women's promotion potential should not be a reason to adjust combat policies; promoting a social agenda should not be a factor; catering to a political lobby should not be a reason. Policies should never be aimed at reaching a quota or making a press release. Military policies should only be developed for one purpose: fighting and winning our nation's wars.

This is why I believe that the right women should continue to serve in combat arms roles under age- and gender-neutral, combat-focused standards.

I wish I had had a female soldier with me in Afghanistan when an Afghan woman approached me begging for help. Armed males menacingly gathered around to heckle and began physically harassing her for talking to me; I tried to help, but the more I tried, the worse it got. After we left, I never saw that woman again; I'm still haunted by what may have happened to her. If I had had a female soldier with me, that situation might have ended very differently.

Are there females in my company who are overweight or cannot pass a fitness test or do a buddy drag or complete a ruck march or finish an obstacle course? Yes, unfortunately. Are there also males in my company who are overweight or cannot do these things? Yes, unfortunately. Is that a problem? Absolutely. But there are also several stars—of both genders—that pull more than their fair share of the weight. Though we encounter myriad obstacles, my first sergeant and I work ceaselessly to train and improve the soldiers that cannot meet the standard and dismiss the soldiers from the Army if they are ultimately unable to do so.

Women can and do bring different skills and perspectives to the table and often approach problems differently. Some women have proven themselves able to demonstrate leadership and articulate new ideas better than some of their male counterparts. Women like Capt. Shaye Haver or Capt. Kris Griest, the first two female Ranger School graduates; or my female executive officer, my highly competent second-in-command; or Rezagul, the Afghan woman who killed twenty-five Taliban fighters; or any of the Army women's rugby players—any of these would undoubtedly make any infantry unit better, stronger, and more lethal. Are they "average" women? No. But they can meet the standard; why ban them from doing so?

Changing a culture is never without headache or heartache. Racial integration of the Army was not easy, either—it had more than its fair share of stutters and missteps, from social isolation to all-black units to segregated facilities. But flawed standards and imperfect implementation are not good reasons to scrap worthy policies. We should not penalize a capable and competent minority of women because the majority may not be qualified to serve in combat arms units; instead, let's fix the real problem so that all of our combat forces adhere to a higher standard.

> *"Many myths, based on stereotype and perpetuated by a minority of 'old and bold' military personnel, are historically unfounded."*

We Shouldn't Believe the Myths About Women in Combat

Leanne K. Simpson

In the following viewpoint, Leanne K. Simpson takes on specific common beliefs about women in combat and explains why she thinks these are myths that should be disregarded. The author brings up some claims not addressed in previous viewpoints, for example, the oft-repeated claims that women are less emotionally stable and that they lack to ability to be violent when necessary. Leanne K. Simpson is a psychologist at the Institute for the Psychology of Elite Performance at Bangor University in the United Kingdom.

"Eight Myths About Women on the Military Frontline—and Why We Shouldn't Believe Them," by Leanne K. Simpson, The Conversation, April 1, 2016. https://theconversation .com/eight-myths-about-women-on-the-military-frontline-and-why-we-shouldnt -believe-them-55594. Licensed under CC BY-ND 4.0.

As you read, consider the following questions:

1. Why will women's supposed physical inferiority soon be irrelevant?
2. At what other stressful jobs have women proved successful?
3. What data does the author use to support her claim that sexual violence against women in the military is not a women's issue?

Although women have proven themselves capable in frontline combat situations—most recently in Iraq and Afghanistan—sceptics argue that this does not demonstrate they are capable of the dirty, exhausting, terrifying and chaotic job that is offensive close combat.

Many myths, based on stereotype and perpetuated by a minority of "old and bold" military personnel, are historically unfounded. However, the findings do not seem to be filtering through—and popular opinion still believes that women are incapable of serving in ground close combat roles. It is time to put these myths to bed once and for all:

1. Women Are Physically Inferior to Men

We have known since the 1980s that direct measures of strength are a more valid qualification criteria than sex and that women are capable of the same level of physical fitness as men of the same size and build. Now, putting that aside, advances in military equipment such as exoskeleton suits are being developed to reduce the effort spent by soldiers while increasing the amount of weight they can carry and the distance they can cover. This will soon make physical inferiority regardless of sex a moot point.

2. Women Lack Violent Tendencies

In truth, women are just as capable of violence as men. Although studies have consistently found that males are more aggressive than females, very little of the research considers the sex of the victim in comparison to the sex of the aggressor. When controlling for this, the sex difference isn't as clear-cut—women are equal to, if not more aggressive than, men in some contexts.

One former female warrant officer in the British Army to whom I spoke for this article said: "Military training ensures that all personnel regardless of sex are capable of aggressive behaviour that is appropriate and proportionate even in high-risk hostile environments."

3. Women Lack the Mental Discipline Required

Women have proven themselves to be mentally formidable, performing highly stressful jobs—for example, as doctors, police officers and pilots—alongside their male counterparts. Research has quashed the sexually dimorphic view of the human brain, instead demonstrating that our brains are highly individualised and mental discipline cannot be discriminated by sex.

4. Women Are Not as Emotionally Stable as Men

Men and women suffer from depression at similar rates, however there is a suicide paradox in which men are more likely to succeed in taking their own lives than women are. Men are also more likely to have substance abuse and addiction problems. Not quite the picture of emotional stability one might assume is needed for comparison.

5. Women Will Be Sexually Assaulted by Male Peers

Military sexual trauma is a concern particularly in the US, where an estimated 20,000 assaults occurred in 2014, against 40% of active-duty female soldiers and 13% of active-duty male soldiers. Based on these percentages it is estimated that 11,400 male and

8,600 female personnel were sexually assaulted in 2014; so, while the proportion of women assaulted is higher, more men were actually victimised—dispelling this misconception that this is a woman's issue.

The US figures include assaults by "other service members, civilians, spouses or others." In the UK, the military police received 225 allegations of rape and sexual assault between 2011 and 2013 from active-duty soldiers against their colleagues.

6. Women Will Jeopardise Unit Cohesion

A 2009 literature review on women in ground close combat roles for the UK's Ministry of Defence found a positive relationship between team cohesion and performance. However, it was unable to make a clear recommendation due to a lack of scientific data examining the effects of women in close combat teams particularly within the UK Armed Forces.

Consequently, the decision was left to "a military judgement that under conditions of high intensity close quarter battle, team cohesion is of such significance that the employment of women in this environment would represent a risk to combat effectiveness with no gain in terms of combat effectiveness to offset it." A disappointing conclusion for equality campaigners considering the review stated there was no scientific evidence to show that women would or would not impact unit cohesion.

A more recent review that aimed to update the 2009 work came up with a different conclusion, finding that gender was not a significant factor in team cohesion. It went on to note that any negative issues related to the integration of women and unit cohesion were short-lived, and could be offset by collective experience and strong leadership—a major factor in how well units perform, rather than the presence or absence of women.

7. Female Military Units Won't Work

There are already examples of many battle-proven all-female units, including the Kurdish Women's Protection Units (YPJ) in Rojava, Kurdistan—the most recent female military unit to capture media attention. The YPJ has been extraordinarily successful, playing a key role during the liberation of Kobani in Syria.

The YPJ have also assisted the Yazidi community, who were trapped on Mount Sinjar in Iraq in 2014. The rescue operation saved thousands of Yazidis who had taken refuge on the mountain and fought thirst and hunger for months, including a large population of women and children who were at risk of being captured and enslaved by Islamic State (IS). For IS, who believe that death at the hands of a woman disqualifies them from Paradise, these women are a formidable threat.

8. Women Can't Perform as Well as Men in the Special Forces

Many countries have made significant progress towards full gender integration in the military, accepting that women should have the same opportunity to serve their country as their male counterparts. However, there seems to be an unequal application of gender equality when it comes to some Special Forces (SF) units.

In December last year, the US military said that all combat jobs will be open to women with no exceptions—but by January it was announced that this "gender-neutral" policy wouldn't include SF units.

SF selection processes are largely a physical aptitude test that is optimised for a male cohort. Arguably this isn't appropriate for current operational requirements. Considering the irregular nature of current operating environments—where frontlines are rarer and enemies don't wear uniforms—it seems that SF units must continually evolve to deal with modern threats. A retired UK Special Forces major told me that: "[21st-century] threats will require a greater reliance on specialists embedded and working within 'traditional' SF structures." They added:

More effective recruitment and retention of women is likely to be an important part of that evolution. In many respects this is back to the future, creating something that looks more like a special operations executive.

There is no shortage of female talent in the military and it is time to use it fully. While not every woman will be capable of serving in ground close combat roles, neither is every man. Access to such roles should be based on competence and qualifications, not determined by a Y chromosome.

> *"From women serving in combat roles, segregation and civil rights, to allowing the LGBT community in its ranks, the military is typically 10–20 years ahead of American society on dispelling certain prejudices."*

The US Has Had an Inconsistent Policy Regarding LGBTQ People in the Military

Rod Powers

In the following viewpoint, Rod Powers traces the evolution of government policy regarding LGBTQ people in the US military, from World War II to the present. As he points out, these policies have changed over the years, depending on the situation. However, in general, the military has been at the vanguard of social progress in the United States. Rod Powers served 22 years in the US military and has since written many articles and books on military life and policy.

"Policies Concerning LGBTQ People in the US Military," by Rod Powers, Dotdash, September 9, 2019. Reprinted by permission.

As you read, consider the following questions:

1. Historically, the US military has relaxed its policies on gay individuals serving in what situations, according to the viewpoint?
2. What was the "Don't Ask, Don't Tell" policy, and why was it implemented?
3. Why was the "Don't Ask, Don't Tell" policy unsatisfactory for LGBTQ service members and LGBTQ people considering joining the military?

Throughout its history, the US Military had an inconsistent policy when it came to gay people in the military. Prior to World War II, there was no written policy barring homosexuals from serving, although sodomy was considered a crime by military law (UCMJ) ever since Revolutionary War times.

Homosexuality Policies in the Korean War and Vietnam War

During World War II, the Korean War, and the Vietnam War, the military defined homosexuality as a mental defect and officially barred homosexuals from serving based on medical criteria. However, when personnel needs increased due to combat, the military developed a habit of relaxing its screening criteria. Many homosexual men and women served honorably during these conflicts. Unfortunately, these periods were short-lived. As soon as the need for combat personnel decreased, the military would involuntarily discharge them.

1982—Complete Ban of Gays in the Military

It wasn't until 1982 that the Department of Defense officially put in writing that "homosexuality was incompatible with military service," when they published a DOD directive stating such. According to a 1992 report by the Government Accounting Office, nearly 17,000 men and women were discharged under this new directive during the 1980s.

The Birth of "Don't Ask, Don't Tell," 1993

By the end of the 1980s, reversing the military's policy was emerging as a priority for advocates of gay and lesbian civil rights. Several lesbian and gay members of the military came out publicly and vigorously challenged their discharges through the legal system. By the beginning of 1993, it appeared that the military's ban on gay personnel would soon be overturned.

President Clinton announced that he intended to keep his campaign promise by eliminating military discrimination based on sexual orientation. But, this didn't sit well with the Republican-controlled Congress. Congressional leaders threatened to pass legislation that would bar homosexuals from serving if Clinton issued an executive order changing the policy.

After lengthy public debate and congressional hearings, the President and Senator Sam Nunn, chair of the Senate Armed Services Committee, reached a compromise which they labeled Don't Ask, Don't Tell, Don't Pursue. Under its terms, military personnel would not be asked about their sexual orientation and would not be discharged simply for being gay. However, having sexual relations, or displaying romantic overtures with members of the same sex, or telling anyone about their sexual orientation is considered "homosexual conduct" under the policy and is a basis for involuntary discharge. This is was known as the "Don't Ask, Don't Tell" law and became the Department of Defense policy.

Changing Times for Society and the Military

At the time, most military leaders and young enlisted (who were forced to live in the barracks with a roommate) took a conservative view about allowing gays to serve openly in the military. But the attitudes of society changed through the next two decades. By 2010, most junior enlisted (the ones who have to live in the barracks),

> ## TRANSGENDER TROOPS BANNED, EVEN THOUGH THE PUBLIC OPPOSES THE BAN
>
> On July 26, 2017, President Trump posted a series of tweets in the early morning hours announcing that "[t]he United States Government will not accept or allow transgender individuals to serve in any capacity in the US Military." The unexpected and callous tweets were swiftly and widely condemned, including by more than 56 retired generals and admirals, as well as prominent Members of Congress from both sides of the aisle. A month after the initial tweets, President Trump issued a formal memorandum detailing the ban and directing Secretary of Defense James Mattis to produce implementation recommendations, which he did in March 2018.
>
> Soon after the announcement of the ban, multiple lawsuits were filed challenging its constitutionality. In response, several federal courts issued injunctions preventing the Trump-Pence Administration from implementing the ban while the cases proceed. However, on January 22, 2019, the Supreme Court lifted the injunctions, allowing the Department of Defense to implement the ban while litigation

today, saw nothing wrong with homosexuality and would not be bothered by serving with those they know to be gay.

Repeal of "Don't Ask, Don't Tell," 2010

In December of 2010, the House and Senate voted in favor to repeal and overturn the policy known as "Don't Ask, Don't Tell." President Obama then signed it into law December 22, 2010. The nation decided that by September 20, 2011, homosexuals would no longer fear discharge from the military by admitting to their sexual preference. Homosexuals have the freedom to serve in the armed forces openly.

Over 13,000 servicemen and women were discharged for being gay while the Don't Ask, Don't Tell policy was in effect. The repeal has prompted many to try and reenlist. Many men and continues, without issuing a ruling on the ban itself. The Administration began implementing the ban on April 12, 2019.

Transgender troops have been serving openly and successfully since 2016, including hundreds who have deployed to combat zones. The Chiefs of Staff to each military branch have testified that there have been no negative impact on readiness. Additionally, data obtained by the Pentagon has shown that the cost of providing medical care to transgender troops has been miniscule. The American Medical Association, American Psychological Association, and American Psychiatric Association all oppose the ban, stating that there is no medical reason transgender troops should be barred from serving.

The policy allowing transgender troops to serve openly did not grant any special exceptions. Transgender service members were held to the exact same rigorous standards as every other service member. They simply were no longer arbitrarily barred from service because of their gender identity.

Polling shows that the majority of Americans in every state and the District of Columbia oppose the Trump-Pence discriminatory ban and support transgender people serving openly in the military.

"Transgender Military Service," The Human Rights Campaign, March 2, 2020.

women who have been serving came out of the closet on various media. Many organizations and groups supporting gay and lesbian military members surfaced and have even organized official public gatherings with the military.

Recognition of Same-Sex Marriages

Following the Supreme Court ruling that struck down the Defense of Marriage Act in 2013, the Department of Defense announced it would extend spousal and family benefits for same-sex marriages that would be the same as those given for traditional marriages.

Transgender Regulations Repealed, 2016

Another frontier was crossed when the ban on service by openly transgender persons in the military was repealed on July 1, 2016. Though in the current administration in 2017, President Trump stated that a goal of his is to not allow transgender men and women to serve in the military. The Department of Defense has yet to change their policy on the proposed ban.

With many controversial public issues, the military has been in the forefront of society throughout history. From women serving in combat roles, segregation and civil rights, to allowing the LGBT community in its ranks, the military is typically 10–20 years ahead of American society on dispelling certain prejudices. It may not be a perfect system 100% of the time, but the cross section of society that is the military in the United States is more lenient and understanding than the rest of the world with certain controversial matters.

As of March 2019, Department of Defense has set not policy to separate transgender service members. Under the new Department of Defense rules, troops and recruits can still identify as transgender. However, they must be their biological sex and use the uniforms, pronouns, and sleeping and bathroom facilities that are appropriate. This affects about 9,000 military members.

| "There are costs of not providing transition-related care, due to potential medical and psychological consequences of its denial."

Medical Care of Transgender Troops Is Too Low to Justify a Ban

Aaron Belkin

One of the common justifications of denying transgender people the right to serve in the military is that their health care costs too much. In the following viewpoint, Aaron Belkin analyzes the cost of such care. Here, he presents his findings and argues that the cost is too low to use as a justification for banning transgender troops. Aaron Belkin is a political science professor at San Francisco State University and director of the Palm Center, an independent research organization.

As you read, consider the following questions:

1. How does the author of this viewpoint describe transition-related care?
2. In what situations might the cost of care be even lower than expected, according to the author's analysis?
3. Why is transition-related care medically necessary?

From the *New England Journal of Medicine*, Aaron Belkin, "Caring for Our Transgender Troops—The Negligible Cost of Transition-Related Care," 373, 12. Copyright © 2015 Massachusetts Medical Society. Reprinted with permission from Massachusetts Medical Society.

On July 13, 2015, US Defense Secretary Ashton Carter announced that the military anticipates lifting its ban on service by transgender persons, those whose gender identity does not match the sex that they were assigned at birth. Although an estimated 12,800 transgender personnel currently serve in the US armed forces, they must conceal their gender identity because military policy bans them from serving and prohibits military doctors from providing transition-related care. Although some transgender people do not change their bodies to match their gender identities, government agencies, courts, and scientists agree that for many, transition-related care (gender-affirming surgery, cross-sex hormone therapy, or both) is medically necessary, and state regulators have found medical exclusions to be indefensible and in some cases unlawfully discriminatory. Yet in response to Carter's announcement, opponents in the Pentagon and beyond expressed concerns about the costs of providing such care.

Having analyzed the cost that the military will incur by providing transition-related care, I am convinced that it is too low to warrant consideration in the current policy debate. Specifically, I estimate that the provision of transition-related care will cost the military $5.6 million annually, or 22 cents per member per month. Of course, the cost will depend on how many transgender personnel serve and utilize care, and estimates are sensitive to certain assumptions, such as the expectation that the military will not become a "magnet" employer for transgender people seeking health care benefits. Though my utilization and cost estimates are quite close to actual data provided by an allied military force, it seems clear that under any plausible estimation method, the cost amounts to little more than a rounding error in the military's $47.8 billion annual health care budget.

My calculations are as follows. In 2014, scholars estimated that 15,500 transgender personnel served in the military out of a total force of 2,581,000, but they included troops who were ineligible for health benefits.[1] Moreover, the military has become smaller in recent years: as of May 31, 2015, a total of 2,136,779 troops served in the Active and Selected Reserve components and were thus eligible for health benefits. Assuming that the number of transgender personnel has declined along with the overall force size, and excluding those serving in Reserve components whose members are ineligible for medical benefits, I estimate that 12,800 transgender troops serve currently and are eligible for health care.

As for the expected utilization of transition-related care, the latest research suggests that among large civilian employers whose insurance plans offer transition-related care including surgery and hormones, an average of 0.044 per thousand employees (one of every 22,727) file claims for such care annually.[2] On the basis of this utilization rate, the military could expect that 94 transgender service members will require transition-related care annually. However, transgender persons are overrepresented in the military by a factor of two—possibly in part because, before attaining self-acceptance, many transgender women (people born biologically male who identify as female) seek to prove to themselves that they are not transgender by joining the military and trying to fit into its hypermasculine culture.[5]

If transgender people are twice as likely to serve in the military as to work for the civilian firms from which the 0.044 figure was derived, then an estimated 188 transgender service members would be expected to require some type of transition-related care annually. It is not possible, on the basis of the available data, to estimate how many will require hormones only, surgery only, or hormones plus surgery.

As an accuracy check, consider the Australian military, which covers the cost of transition-related care: over a 30-month period, 13 Australian troops out of a full-time force of 58,000 underwent gender transition—an average of 1 service member out of 11,154 per year.[3] If the Australian rate were applicable to the US military, the Pentagon could expect 192 service members to undergo gender transition annually.

To estimate the cost of care, note that under insurance plans offered to University of California employees and their dependents, the average cost of transition-related care (surgery, hormones, or both) per person needing treatment was $29,929 over 6.5 years.[4] This estimate was derived from 690,316 total person-years of coverage, a sample arguably large enough to justify extrapolation to other settings.[4] By comparison, over a 30-month period, the Australian military paid US $287,710 for transition-related care for 13 service members, or $22,132 per person requiring care.[3]

Under these utilization-rate and cost-per-claimant estimates, providing transition-related care to the 188 military personnel expected to require it annually would cost an estimated $5.6 million per year, or $438 per transgender service member per year, or 22 cents per member per month. If the Australian military's annual cost of transition-related care were applied to the US armed forces, the Pentagon could expect to pay $4.2 million per year to provide such care.

Actual costs could be lower than expected, because transition-related care has been proven to mitigate serious conditions including suicidality that, left untreated, impose costs on the military, and addressing symptoms might conceivably improve job performance as well. There are costs, in other words, of not providing transition-related care, due to potential medical and psychological consequences of its denial, paired with the requirement to live a closeted life. In addition, the $29,929 cost-per-claimant estimate was derived from private-sector care, but the military provides care more efficiently than civilian systems do. Although the military might outsource some transition surgeries to private providers, many transition surgeries are well within the skill set of its reconstructive surgeons. Finally, transgender service members may be less likely than civilians to seek transition-related care, owing to hostile command climates or an unwillingness to interrupt military service.

In contrast, actual costs will be higher if the military covers more procedures than the insurance plans from which the $29,929 estimate was derived. In addition, costs will be higher if transition-related care is offered to family members and dependents. Finally, if transgender civilians join the military in order to obtain care, costs will be higher than estimated. Military recruiters have used the promise of health care benefits to entice civilians to enlist, and if transition-related coverage motivates outstanding transgender candidates to serve, that is not necessarily problematic. That said, civilian insurance plans increasingly cover transition-related care, which reduces the incentive to join the armed forces to obtain care. And low utilization rates reported by civilian firms offering such care may suggest that few transgender persons obtain civilian employment for that purpose. If so, it would be difficult to imagine that large numbers would seek to join the military to obtain such care, given the multiyear service obligations they would incur.

Some observers may object to the concept that the military should pay for transition-related care, but doctors agree that such care is medically necessary. And though costs can be high per treated person, they are low as a percentage of total health spending, similar to the cost of many other treatments that the military provides. Even if actual costs exceed these estimates on a per-capita basis for persons requiring care, the total cost of providing transition-related care will always have a negligible effect on the military health budget because of the small number treated and the cost savings that the provision of such care will yield. The financial cost of transition-related care, in short, is too low to matter.

Endnotes

1. Gates G, Herman J. Transgender military service in the United States. Los Angeles: Williams Institute, 2014.
2. Herman J. Costs and benefits of providing transition-related health care coverage in employee health benefits plans: findings from a survey of employers. Los Angeles: Williams Institute, 2013.
3. 9News (NineMSN). Australians hit with $648,000 bill for military's gender reassignment and breast enhancement surgeries. June 9, 2015 (http://www.9news .com.au/national/2015/06/09/05/44/taxpayers-funding-adf-breast-enhancements -and-gender-reassignment. opens in new tab).
4. Economic impact assessment: gender nondiscrimination in health insurance. Los Angeles: State of California Department of Insurance, 2012.
5. Brown GR. Transsexuals in the military: flight into hypermasculinity. *Arch Sex Behav* 1988;17:527-537.

> "History is rich with people who demonstrated behaviors that did not conform to gender norms. It was their ability to do their jobs that mattered. Shouldn't the same be true for transgender service members?"

The Ability to Do the Job Is All That Matters

Jay Caputo

The author of the previous viewpoint detailed why the costs of transition-related health care for transgender troops was minimal but did not go on to make any further claims about whether or not transgender Americans should be allowed to serve. In the following viewpoint, Jay Caputo explains why any citizen who is both fit and willing should be allowed to serve. Jay Caputo is a captain in the United States Coast Guard.

As you read, consider the following questions:

1. Why might it be difficult to make a "fact-based assessment" of the issue of transgender service members?
2. How does the author compare gender reassignment surgery to cosmetic surgery?
3. What surgeries related to transition are not paid for by the military?

Reprinted from PROCEEDINGS with Permission, Copyright © 2017 US Naval Institute. www.usni.org.

I n response to the 25 August 2017 presidential memorandum "Military Service by Transgender Individuals," the Department of Defense is developing an implementation plan that will address transgender individuals currently serving in the US military, as well as the accession of transgender individuals into the military. With Secretary of Defense James Mattis's recommendation to the White House expected in the next few months, the department is rightly focused on developing a plan that will "promote military readiness, lethality, and unit cohesion, with due regard for budgetary constraints and consistent with applicable law."[1]

The topic of transgender service sparks a wide array of passionate responses. For many people, who may never have (knowingly) interacted with a transgender person, this may be new and unfamiliar territory. Unfortunately, there are numerous myths, stereotypes, and even lies about transgender individuals intermingled with the facts, which can make this topic confusing. What information is accurate and what is "fake news"? What does it mean to be transgender? Are transgender members fit to serve? How does transition affect military service? What are the costs? How will this affect nontransgender members in a unit? Add the various cultural, social, political, media, and religious perspectives and the ability to make an impartial, fact-based assessment of the situation has become extremely difficult. This article aims to separate fact from fiction to assess whether transgender members should be allowed to serve in the military.

"T" Primer

"Trans" gender (meaning "across" gender) refers to persons who do not identify with the sex they are assigned at birth—for example, an individual who physically looks female and is assigned the gender of female at birth but identifies as male. The American Psychiatric Association notes that "gender nonconformity is not in itself a mental disorder." In fact, scientists have discovered that transgender brains more closely resemble the brains of the gender identified with than the gender assigned at birth.[2] The body does not match the brain. Transgender individuals were born into the incorrect bodies.

The term "identify" is used, but this is not a choice. Mentally, transgender persons are their identified gender, only their physical bodies do not match. Though often lumped together in the term "LGBT" (with lesbian, gay, and bisexual), transgender has nothing to do with a person's sexual orientation. The gender you identify with has no relation to whom you are attracted to. Closeted transgender persons work extremely hard to keep their condition hidden. Imagine waking up in a body of the opposite gender. It would take effort to get dressed, act appropriately, and somehow make it through the day playing the part. Then you would go to sleep and start over again the next day, and the next, for the rest of your life. Over time, this creates stress, which is medically diagnosed as Gender Dysphoria (GD).[3] A diagnosis of GD means the person is debilitated by their dissatisfaction with their physical body and the label they were assigned at birth. Some with GD manage to live with a mismatched body their entire lives, others become depressed, and for some it is so bad they become suicidal.[4] Each person's response is unique.

The treatment for GD is to "transition" to the sex with which one identifies. For individuals who are transitioning—"coming out" to live openly as their gender identity—this typically means changing hair, grooming, and clothing styles. Most, but not all, pursue a variety of medical options to make their physical features match their gender identities, including laser hair removal, hormone replacement therapy, and surgical intervention.

Fitness to Serve

Where do transgender persons fall related to "fitness to serve"? Any person with a male body must meet male service standards; anyone with a female body must meet female standards. Transgender persons who can meet the standards of their physical body are fit for service. The standards remain unchanged. Those who meet the standards can serve; those who do not cannot. Transgender personnel are medically and physically fit to serve; they meet standards and serve today. The only new issue involves transitioning, which is the most poorly understood aspect of whether transgender persons are fit to serve.

Culturally, we routinely alter our bodies to correct what we perceive to be a defect or simply for aesthetic preference—everything from cleft lip or palate surgery to laser eye surgery to cosmetic surgery. When physical issues are noticed at birth, they often are corrected while the child is young. However, there is no scan or test to know if individuals are transgender. It takes time, as they grow, for them to fully understand why they feel different. The mismatch of body with gender identity cannot be detected for many years, at which time societal pressures can keep individuals from addressing the mismatch until later in life.

Many types of physical "defects" can be corrected and meet military standards. A service member who is injured in combat, a car accident, or while playing sports on the weekend is provided medical treatment and allowed time to recover. Members who may temporarily be unfit for deployment because of injury, illness, medical condition, or mental health issues routinely are treated with medication, surgery, therapy, or other intervention and brought back to full fitness for duty. Having GD is no different; it is correctable through treatment by transitioning.

Service members have a wide array of health-care issues the military treats to ensure fitness for duty, including high blood pressure, cancer, musculoskeletal injuries, high cholesterol, concussions, and mental health issues. For a few members, their medical issue is GD. Treatment generally includes counseling, changes to grooming, clothing, and lifestyle, medication to alter hormone levels, and a variety of surgical procedures to make permanent alterations to the body. Depending on the nature of the deployment and the severity of the GD diagnosis, members may be able to complete some of their transition while deployed and take care of other aspects between deployments.

What if someone could not get their prescription medication while deployed? Would it hinder their readiness? Military members deploy worldwide every day while taking the same medications transgender persons use, just for different reasons. Transgender members can still operate and function without their medication, the same as women who are unable to get birth control pills refilled while deployed. While the situation is not ideal, it would not limit a person's ability to perform their duties.

The cost of transgender surgery often is cited as a reason transgender members should not serve. First, not all transgender people get surgeries, but for those who do, let's examine the costs. If a transgender person chooses to have sex reassignment surgery, estimated costs range between $20,000 and $30,000.[5] In Canada, 19 service members completed sex reassignment surgery between 2008 and 2015 for a total cost of $319,000, according to a Canadian broadcast news service.[6] Other surgeries to refine the person's appearance—face lifts, body contouring, hair removal, etc.—are paid for by the member. Hormone replacement drugs costs around $30 per month and doctor visits about $100 per month, about the same for other medications. Total costs are estimated at $2.4 million to $8.4 million, or .04 percent to .14 percent of an annual military health-care budget of more than $6 billion.[7] Knee replacement surgery costs on average $49,500 per knee, and recovery time is 7 to 12 weeks.[8] The recovery time for the most extensive transgender surgery is 6 to 8 weeks. The down time for many less invasive procedures may be a week or less. Also, people who opt for surgical interventions require less medication or are eligible for longer term solutions, such as subdermal inserts or patches.

The medical costs to return highly trained military members to duty pale in comparison to the time, money, and effort required to replace them, which is why the military works to get personnel back into a medically fit status rather than simply discharging everyone who gets sick or injured. So why not provide treatment to cure a medical diagnosis such as GD? The difference is many people are not educated about transgender health needs, and social stigmas get in the way.

The key issue for transgender members related to fitness for service is the transition period, which is about 12 to 18 months— similar to the time required for shoulder rotator cuff surgery or to bring a pregnancy to term. Within that time frame, there will be periods when they are not fit for full duty if pursuing surgeries, but working with commands when scheduling these procedures can minimize disruption to the unit. Once the transition is complete, which includes meeting fitness standards for the new physical gender, the gender marker would be changed in the Defense Enrollment Eligibility Reporting System and the person would be available for worldwide deployment.

If a transgender person meets standards, wants to join, and already has transitioned, there is no down time for transition and no costs for surgical interventions.

Willingness to Serve

History is rich with people who demonstrated behaviors that did not conform to gender norms. In the early 1400s, Joan of Arc wore men's clothing and armor and led a military campaign. She was tried for heresy and burned at the stake. One of the charges was cross dressing. Today she is considered a heroine of France. Admiral Zheng He was a Muslim eunuch who fought numerous battles for the Chinese emperor and was renowned for his military ability and leadership. Today he is honored every year on China's national maritime day. There are other examples of people who varied from stereotypical gender behavior who were valued for their character and achievements, not their appearance or the status of their genitalia. It was their ability to do their jobs that mattered.

The same is true today. The military has invested millions of dollars to train transgender members, and many have served proudly or are serving in every field: intelligence experts, administrative specialists, war zone linguists, combat infantry, health service professionals, and commanding officers.

The "Real" Issue

If transgender persons meet service standards, currently serve with honor, and the costs to transition are comparable (or less) than many other medical issues the military covers, why should they be removed from service or not be allowed to join? Why has accepting transitioning or post-transition members been so divisive?

Many do not understand what it means to be transgender. They think it is a mental illness (it is not). They think it is a choice (it is not). They think the costs are exorbitant (they are not). They worry transgender persons will flood into the military for a taxpayer-funded sex change (not realistic). Once the myths are debunked and the facts established, what is left?

Transphobia is the intense dislike of or prejudice against transgender people. No matter the facts, some people simply do not like the idea of serving with someone who does not fit their definition of "normal." People who argue against transgender service often say it disrupts good order and discipline, arguing that service members are uncomfortable with the presence of transgender people. Whether for bathrooms, barracks, or showers, this argument has been used before—to keep African Americans, women, and LGB members out of the service. Before each of these groups was allowed into the military, there were many who cried that doing so would erode morale, unit cohesion, esprit de corps, and effectiveness. Yet, when they were allowed in, the sky did not fall and units did not lose their effectiveness. Instead, the military gained more warfighters. Imagine our military today if we had listened to those fears and barred any of these groups from service.

National acceptance is growing. A recent Pew poll found nearly 90 percent of Americans know someone who is LGB.[9] According to a 2016 Harris poll, while only 16 percent of adults know a transgender person, that number is higher among millennials. In addition, the Harris study found that 1 in 5 millennials self-identify with the LGBT community.[10] Nearly half of US military members are 25 years old or younger, and nearly three-fourths are under 30, or basically millennials.[11] The future of the military is our young recruits, and data shows they are more open and accepting of LGBT members. And as more transgender persons feel comfortable coming out, more people will know a transgender person and their attitudes likely will change, which is what happened when LGB members started coming out in larger numbers.

If you want to know how a transgender person will affect a unit, ask the members of a unit that has a transgender member. They likely will tell you this is a non-issue. There is no impact on readiness or unit morale. And the issue of bathrooms, showers, etc., can be easily resolved with unit-level solutions. While new and awkward at first, open, honest conversation with command leadership quickly dispels the matter. Many have opinions as to how this will affect units, but only those who serve with transgender persons truly know.

There also is discussion of a "compromise" that would allow transgender persons currently in the military to continue to serve but not cover the medical costs for transitions or post-transition sustainment. Nor would new transgender members be allowed to enter the service. This will not work. We learned from "Don't Ask, Don't Tell" that this type of "it's okay so long as we don't know about it" policy does not work. First, the service always will have transgender members. Many may not realize or accept they are transgender until years after they join; others initially will be content joining based on their gender assignment. The stress of living in a body that is not "right" will take its toll, however, and many of these individuals will be diagnosed with GD. Do we kick them out? Worse, do they fail to seek help for fear of discharge and end up in severe depression or even commit suicide, as happens now? How would that affect unit readiness? We cannot "closet" transgender persons to allow them to serve, just as "closeting" LGB members did not work.

We must remain focused on investing in our warfighters and not be distracted by society's transition through familiar phases that eventually will result in acceptance and integration of the transgender community. Removing transgender service members will break a bond with the service members and their families, just to support a goal of making a few soldiers, sailors, Marines, airmen, and Coast Guardsmen "comfortable." This is a waste of taxpayers' investment in otherwise skilled warfighters. Let's learn from history and skip the part of this societal cycle where we fall victim to the "doom and gloom" of the naysayers. Our workforce has proven time again they grow stronger through diversity and inclusion.

The Nation Needs Transgender Service

Being "comfortable" is not a luxury the nation can afford. The world is full of dark and terrible things: cyber attacks, hurricanes, depleted food resources, terrorists, and threat of nuclear war. To ensure it can defend the nation, the military needs eligible, willing Americans to fill its ranks. Unfortunately, the number of people eligible for military service is shrinking. More than 70 percent of the population between 17 and 24 years of age is unable to meet eligibility requirements.[12] Of those eligible to join, many are recruited by other employers or simply are not interested in serving.

Transgender persons are ready, willing, and able. Not counting the United States, 18 countries today allow transgender persons to serve.[13] They are a normal part of society and have played critical roles throughout history, whether we knew it or not. Many have served or are currently serving; future generations similarly will step up and want to serve. The military values diversity, not for demographics themselves, but for diversity of thought. Different perspectives, backgrounds, and experience, including those unique to transgender members, all contribute to an ability to see problems differently and devise creative solutions. The nation needs the best, strongest, most lethal military possible, and transgender service fully supports that goal. Arguments about costs, bathrooms, unit cohesion, and social engineering are red herrings.

History is rich with people who demonstrated behaviors that did not conform to gender norms. It was their ability to do their jobs that mattered. Shouldn't the same be true for transgender service members? Secretary Mattis summed this up nicely during his January 2017 confirmation hearing: "We need to open the door to all who are eligible and wish to serve."[14]

Endnotes

1. "Statement by Secretary of Defense Jim Mattis on Military Service by Transgender Individuals," news release, Department of Defense, 29 August 2017; www.defense .gov/News/News-Releases/News-Release-View/Article/1294351/statement-by -secretary-of-defense-jim-mattis-on-military-service-by-transgender/.

2. Robin Marantz Henig, "How Science Is Helping Us Understand Gender," *National Geographic*, January 2017, www.nationalgeographic.com/magazine/2017/01/how -science-helps-us-understand-gender-identity/.

3. *Diagnostic and Statistical Manual of Mental Disorders 5* (Arlington, VA: American Psychiatric Association, 2013), www.psychiatry.org/psychiatrists/practice/dsm.

4. Ibid. Forty-one percent of transgender adults have attempted suicide.

5. "How Much Does the US Military Actually Spend on Transgender Solders?" *Forbes*, 27 July 2017, www.forbes.com/sites/quora/2017/07/27/how-much-does-the-u-s -military-actually-spend-on-transgender-soldiers/#600ef9fcca6e.

6. Kathleen Harris, "Canada Promotes Recruitment of Transgender Troops as Donald Trump Imposes Military Ban," CBC News, 26 July 2017, www.cbc.ca/news /politics/canada-transgender-military-trump-ban-1.4222787.

7. Doug Irving, "Transgender Troops: Fit to Serve," RAND Review, 18 August 2015, www .rand.org/blog/rand-review/2016/08/transgender-troops-fit-to-serve.html.

8. Samuel Greengard, "Understanding Knee Replacement Costs: What's on the Bill?" Healthline.com, 23 October 2017, www.healthline.com/health/total-knee -replacement-surgery/understanding-costs.

9. Pew Research Center, "Where the Public Stands on Religious Liberty vs. Nondiscrimination," 28 September 2016. 10. "Accelerating Acceptance 2017," survey conducted by Harris Poll on behalf of GLAAD, 30 March 2017, www.glaad. org/publications/accelerating-acceptance-2017 GLAAD Transgender Media Program; www.glaad.org/transgender.

11. 2014 Demographics Profile of the Military Community, Department of Defense.

12. John Grady, "Panel: Pentagon Facing Future Recruiting Challenge Due to Lack of Candidates," USNI News, 12 October 2017, https://news.usni .org/2017/10/12/panel-pentagon-facing-future-recruiting-challenge-due-lack -candidates#more-28748.

13. Paul LeBlanc, "The Countries That Allow Transgender Troops to Serve in Their Armed Forces," CNN.com, 27 July 2017, http://www.cnn.com/2017/07/27/us/world -transgender-ban-facts/.

14. James N. Mattis, "Senate Armed Services Committee Nomination Hearing Statement," www.armed-services.senate.gov/imo/media/doc/Mattis_01-12-17.pdf.

| "While some of the Karakal female
soldiers could possibly be successful
infantry soldiers, there are general
inherent physical obstacles."

Females May Face Challenges in Regular Infantry Units

Aharon S. Finestone, et al.

In the following excerpted viewpoint, Aharon S. Finestone, Charles Milgrom, Ran Yanovich, Rachel Evans, Naama Constantini, and Daniel S. Moran present results of their research study on the fitness of women in the military. The Israeli military was chosen as a subject because Israel is the only nation with mandatory military service for women as well as men, and women there have served in combat for many years, providing a rich data set. The researchers are affiliated with several universities in Israel. Aharon S. Finestone is affiliated with the Department of Orthopaedic Surgery.

As you read, consider the following questions:

1. Why did the researchers choose to study Israeli soldiers?
2. Why did fewer women leave the service for medical reasons even though their rate of injury was higher?
3. What limitations of the study do the authors point out?

"Evaluation of the Performance of Females as Light Infantry Soldiers," by Aharon S. Finestone, Charles Milgrom, Ran Yanovich, Rachel Evans, Naama Constantini, Daniel S. Moran, BioMed Research International, August 18, 2014. https://doi .org/10.1155/2014/572953. Licensed under CC BY 3.0.

Opposition to women serving in military combat positions has come both from within the armed forces and from groups in the general society. The arguments are many, including the position that women are not able to adequately perform combat duties. Beginning in the 1970s, Canada, the USA, Taiwan, Israel, New Zealand, and a few European nations gradually began to allow women to serve in more active combat roles. Of these countries, only Israel has compulsory military service for women. The performance of women in these active combat roles has not been well documented and publicized. Military studies have found that female stress fracture risk and overuse injury risk are greater than those of males doing the same training.[1,2] Other studies have focused on identifying gender specific risk factors for overuse injuries in the military.[3-5]

Measurement of the professional performance of combat soldiers is multifactorial. Dropout from combat units can be considerable. It can be secondary to acute injuries, overuse injuries, lack of motivation, sociological reasons, or psychological factors. Several studies have focused on the attrition of females in the armed forces.[6-10] During USArmy Basic Combat Training, the medical discharge rate for males is 3.3 percent as compared to 8.7 percent for females.[11] At one year, the attrition rate among female US Marine Corp recruits was reported to be 17 percent.[6] The overall attrition rate of female soldiers in the US Marine Corp has been reported to be 1.6 times higher than that of males.[7]

In 1995, the Israel Supreme Court ruled that the Israel Ministry of Defense policy of not allowing women entrance into the Israel Air Force pilot's course was solely based on gender and, therefore, constituted unlawful discrimination. This decision initiated radical changes in the combat active service opportunities for women in the Israel Defense Forces (IDF). Today, women serve in combat roles in many IDF units including the light infantry brigade Karakal, antiaircraft units, the Home Front Command, and the Border Police, in the Navy and in the Air Force.

In view of the controversy about females serving in combat positions, we undertook a study to compare the long-term performance of females and males in the mixed gender light infantry brigade of the Israeli Defense Forces. We report the results of a prospective study of the incidences of their overuse injuries, attrition, and completion of officers' course over the course of their three years of compulsory service.

[…]

Discussion

Female soldiers of Karakal had a high rate of attrition, with only seventy-two percent remaining as combat soldiers throughout their three years of military service. This retention rate, however, was in fact higher than that of male Karakal soldiers. From this standpoint, the program of female service in the mixed gender light infantry unit Karakal can be considered a success.

From a physical standpoint, the females in Karakal, when compared to the males, began their training at a physiological disadvantage. Their O_2max measurements and time for a 2 km run were poorer than those of the males. O_2max in itself is known to be a poor prediction of run performance. The velocity and duration at which subjects can operate at their O_2max provide better indications of performance. Females were able to do less situps and pushups than males at the beginning of basic training. This deficit remained even after 14 weeks of basic training. The females were also shorter and weighed less than the males. This put them at a disadvantage to the males because they used the same equipment and carried the same base loads while training.[26] The females sustained a 21-percent incidence of stress fractures versus a 2-percent incidence for the males. With the exception of stress fractures and anterior knee pain, which were higher in females, there was no difference in the incidence of the other types of overuse injuries between females and males. In spite of the high incidence of stress fractures and the physical and physiological differences between the women and men of Karakal, their attrition rates because of medical reasons were the same.

The attrition rate for males in Karakal was higher than that of the females principally because of drop out for psychological reasons. The psychological variables specifically measured in this study do not fully explain this large difference. One reason may be because the females in Karakal volunteered specifically for service in Karakal while the males were assigned to the unit from the general pool of males designated for combat service. For females, Karakal is one of the most prestigious army combat units in which they could serve, but, for males, it is one of the least prestigious combat units in which they can serve. The IDF has several systems for evaluating recruits prior to induction. There was no statistically significant difference in the preinduction psychotechnical scores and quality scores between the women and men of Karakal. The psychotechnical scores of the Karakal soldiers were lower than those of regular IDF infantry soldiers. Both the female and male Karakal attrition rates were much higher those of regular IDF infantry soldiers, who have more arduous training. Neither of the psychotechnical nor quality scores were predictors of attrition in this study.

Discharge rates among female American Marine Corp recruits, based on 1999-2000 data, have been reported to be 11.2 percent in basic training, with a one year attrition rate of 17.1 percent.[7] This compares to the 24-percent attrition rate for the females of Karakal at 18 months. Unlike the female Marines, most of the Karakal females who left their unit continued to serve but in noncombat positions. In another American Marine Corp study, based on data from 1997, the female discharge rate was 18.2 percent and the male rate was 11.9 percent during 63 days of Marine Corp basic training at Parris Island.[6]

In the current study, 5 percent of the females and 1 percent of the males completed officer's course and became officers. The IDF is different from the American Army in the fact that officers begin as regular soldiers and therefore data cannot be compared.

Those who are identified during their training as being good officer candidates are offered the chance to take an officer's course. Being an officer also requires the soldier to serve for an additional year and not all candidates are willing to do so. About 10% of soldiers in IDF regular infantry units complete officer's course. Since the IDF relies heavily on reserve soldiers, the number of recruits who continue to serve in the reserves after completing mandatory service is important. In this study, 60 percent of both the males and females did reserve army service. This compares with more than 80 percent of regular infantry soldiers.

While this study indicates that women have successfully performed the role of light infantry soldiers in the IDF Karakal unit, the results should not be extrapolated to conclude that they would be similarly successful in a regular infantry unit. While infantry soldiers are expected to be able to carry equipment and supplies sufficient for several days of marching and combat 15–20 kilometers beyond enemy lines, light infantry are not. They are only expected to be able to march 4–5 kilometers with limited combat equipment. They perform most missions and patrols using vehicles. A further difference is the level of fitness. Only 48% of the females and 52% of the males in Karakal reached fitness levels at the end of basic training that would have allowed them to pass minimum IDF infantry soldier standards. The mean O_2max of the females at the end of basic training (36.8 mL·kg^{-1}·min^{-1}) was lower than the norm for females of their age with average fitness (43 mL·kg^{-1}·min^{-1}).[27]

While some of the Karakal female soldiers could possibly be successful infantry soldiers, there are general inherent physical obstacles. Females have inherently only 70 percent of the lower body strength and 30–50 percent of the upper body strength of comparable sized males.[28] Also, because of hormonal differences, females doing strength training build less muscle bulk than males.[29] Identifying females who could successfully serve in IDF infantry units would require intensive screening and include physical fitness and exertion tests, similar to those required before admission to more elite IDF infantry units. This is especially necessary because while the female recruits in Karakal were volunteers for their unit, most of them did little prior physical activity to prepare themselves for the physical challenges of infantry service.[27]

This paper has several limitations. The study compares the performance of females to that of males serving as light infantry soldiers. The study is observational and, therefore, the cohorts could not be matched in any way. The females in Karakal are volunteers to the unit while the males are assigned. The unit has high prestige for the females and low prestige for the males. This results in group bias but does not invalidate the group comparison which is between females and a male cohort who ordinarily serve in such a unit. It does not invalidate the study conclusion that the females perform at least as good as the males in the Karakal unit. Another study weakness is that because the data is pooled from several induction groups there may be variations in methods between groups. Additionally, not all tests were performed on all subjects. This is because, on any individual assessment day, soldiers may have been on limited duty or away from their unit on other assignments. The study supplemented data gathered by the orthopaedic surgeons in the field during basic training by computerized patient records. The active surveillance by the orthopaedists could have led to higher reported injury rates than those which are usually reported.

We conclude that, in general, female participation in the mixed gender light infantry Karakal unit is a success. Females are able to fulfill successfully the combat role of a light infantry soldier. Female soldiers in the unit have lower attrition rates than the males. The higher female incidence of overuse injuries and their lower physical fitness than the males throughout all stages of the Karakal training might represent an impediment to them performing the more arduous training and duties of regular infantry soldiers.

References

1. N. S. Bell, T. W. Mangione, D. Hemenway, P. J. Amoroso, and B. H. Jones, "High injury rates among female Army trainees: a function of gender?" *American Journal of Preventive Medicine*, vol. 18, no. 3, pp. 141–146, 2000.

2. A. Gam, L. Goldstein, Y. Karmon et al., "Comparison of stress fractures of male and female recruits during basic training in the Israeli anti-aircraft forces," *Military Medicine*, vol. 170, no. 8, pp. 710–712, 2005.

3. B. H. Jones, M. W. Bovee, J. M. Harris III, and D. N. Cowan, "Intrinsic risk factors for exercise-related injuries among male and female army trainees," *The American Journal of Sports Medicine*, vol. 21, no. 5, pp. 705–710, 1993.

4. J. Knapik, S. J. Montain, S. McGraw, T. Grier, M. Ely, and B. H. Jones, "Stress fracture risk factors in basic combat training," *International Journal of Sports Medicine*, vol. 33, no. 11, pp. 940–946, 2012.

5. M. J. Rauh, C. A. Macera, D. W. Trone, R. A. Shaffer, and S. K. Brodine, "Epidemiology of stress fracture and lower-extremity overuse injury in female recruits," *Medicine & Science in Sports & Exercise*, vol. 38, no. 9, pp. 1571–1577, 2006.

6. L. M. Pollack, C. B. Boyer, K. Betsinger, and M. Shafer, "Predictors of one-year attrition in female Marine Corps recruits," *Military Medicine,* vol. 174, no. 4, pp. 382–391, 2009.

7. J. Wolfe, K. Turner, M. Caulfield et al., "Gender and trauma as predictors of military attrition: a study of marine corps recruits," *Military Medicine*, vol. 170, no. 12, pp. 1037–1043, 2005.

8. B. P. Bergman and S. A. S. J. Miller, "Equal opportunities, equal risks? Overuse injuries in female military recruits," *Journal of Public Health Medicine*, vol. 23, no. 1, pp. 35–39, 2001.

9. J. J. Knapik, K. G. Hauret, J. L. Lange, and B. Jovag, "Retention in service of recruits assigned to the army physical fitness test enhancement program in basic combat training," *Military Medicine*, vol. 168, no. 6, pp. 490–492, 2003.

10. J. J. Knapik, S. Darakjy, K. G. Hauret et al., "Increasing the physical fitness of low-fit recruits before basic combat training: an evaluation of fitness, injuries, and training outcomes," *Military Medicine*, vol. 171, no. 1, pp. 45–54, 2006.

11. W. E. Siri, "The gross composition of the body," *Advances in Biological and Medical Physics*, vol. 4, pp. 239–280, 1956.

26. N. Constantini, A. S. Finestone, N. Hod et al., "Equipment modification is associated with fewer stress fractures in female Israel border police recruits," *Military Medicine*, vol. 175, no. 10, pp. 799–804, 2010.

27. E. Shvartz and R. C. Reibold, "Aerobic fitness norms for males and females aged 6 to 75 years: a review," *Aviation Space and Environmental Medicine,* vol. 61, no. 1, pp. 3–11, 1990.

28. J. H. Wilmore, "The application of science to sport: physiological profiles of male and female athletes," *Canadian Journal of Applied Sport Sciences*, vol. 4, no. 2, pp. 103–115, 1979.

29. C. H. Brown and J. H. Wilmore, "The effects of maximal resistance training on the strength and body composition of women athletes," *Medicine & Science in Sports & Exercise*, vol. 6, no. 3, pp. 174–177, 1974.

Periodical and Internet Sources Bibliography

The following articles have been selected to supplement the diverse views presented in this chapter.

Jessica Evans, "The Navy Initially Denied Grace Hopper's Enlistment. Then She Revolutionized Computers," *We Are the Mighty*, July 29, 2020. https://www.wearethemighty.com/history/grace-hopper -commodore?rebelltitem=1#rebelltitem1

Necko L. Fanning, "I Thought I Could Serve as an Openly Gay Man in the Army. Then Came the Death Threats," *New York Times Magazine*, April 10, 2019. https://www.nytimes.com/2019/04/10 /magazine/lgbt-military-army.html

Carrie H. Kennedy, "On Being a Woman in the Military," *Psychology Today*, March 24, 2020. https://www.psychologytoday.com/us /blog/alpha-blog-charlie/202003/being-woman-in-the-military

Meghann Myers, "LGBT Service Members Are Allowed to Be Out and Proud, but a Fear of Repercussions Persists," *Military Times*, June 15, 2020. https://www.militarytimes.com/news/your -military/2020/06/15/lgbt-service-members-are-allowed-to-be -out-and-proud-but-a-fear-of-repercussions-persists/

Lori Robinson and Michael E. O'Hanlon, "Women Warriors: The Ongoing Story of Integrating and Diversifying the American Armed Forces," Brookings, May 2020. https://www.brookings .edu/essay/women-warriors-the-ongoing-story-of-integrating -and-diversifying-the-armed-forces/

Heather Marie Stur, "Donald Trump's 'Trans Ban' Reverses More Than 70 Years of Military Integration," *Washington Post,* January 29, 2019. https://www.washingtonpost.com/outlook/2019/01/29 /donald-trumps-trans-ban-reverses-more-than-years-military -integration/

Avivah Wittenberg-Cox, "The Best Defense? How About More Women in the Military?" *Forbes*, April 30, 2020. https://www .forbes.com/sites/avivahwittenbergcox/2020/04/30 /the-best-defense-how-about-more-women-in-the -military/#4d3036cd7bdc

OPPOSING
VIEWPOINTS®
SERIES

CHAPTER 4

Does the US Do Enough for Its Veterans?

Chapter Preface

I n this chapter, we will shift from examining arguments about the composition of and financial support for the military to discussions of what the United States does, or should do, for the men and women who have served in our wars. In short, are we doing enough for returning war veterans, given the sacrifices they make for America?

Some authors here think we're doing fine; others point out ways we could do much better. As it did in earlier chapters, the discussion often touches on—or at least hints at—the often vexed relationship between civilians and the military.

For the most part, the discussions in this chapter center on health care. The United States Veterans Health Administration (VHA), a branch of the US Department of Veterans Affairs (VA), is the government agency in charge of providing health care for veterans. As such, it is the largest integrated health care system in the United States. The VHA operates more than 1,200 health care facilities. Over the years, there has been a big debate about how effective and efficient the VHA is. These viewpoints address that issue from a variety of perspectives. While several authors provide actual data about the VHA's care, much of the discussion comes back to politics and differing economic theories.

And the discussion occasionally comes back to the citizenry's own feelings about war, the military, and the responsibility owed to those who serve by those who don't. As one author points out, decisions we make about caring for veterans may have as much to do with our own psychological health as it does with the health of returning warriors.

> *"Civilians ought to support veterans and help close the civil-military divide, at least in part by learning more about our military and, in turn, helping to carry the burdens of war."*

Americans Don't Do Enough for Retired Soldiers

Ethan Walker

In the following viewpoint, Ethan Walker opens with the tragic story of a troubled veteran. While the author points out this veteran's situation is rare, he does argue that as much as Americans claim to value members of the military—and as much as many organizations do—they don't do nearly enough to help those veterans when they return from battle. At the time of this writing, Ethan Walker was a recent graduate of the University of California–Berkeley and an intern with New America's Future of Property Rights program.

"How Americans Can Do More for Retired Soldiers," by Ethan Walker, The Social Justice Foundation, April 5, 2018. Reprinted by permission.

As you read, consider the following questions:

1. What examples does this author give of things "not going well" regarding US veterans?
2. What are good indicators for the well-being of veterans, according to the author?
3. What does the author suggest that civilians can do for veterans, and why does he think it is important that civilians do so?

In March, Albert Wong—a decorated Army veteran who fought in Afghanistan—killed three former caretakers and himself after an hours-long hostage standoff at Pathway Home, a non-profit that provides clinical, educational, and professional support to veterans transitioning back into the civilian world.

Details regarding Wong's background and possible motives are sure to come out in the weeks ahead, but current reports already point to some potentially troubling indicators. Wong's recent expulsion from the program due to threats made toward one of the women killed in the standoff, as well as comments from those who knew about his struggle to re-adjust after leaving the military (his former guardian stated that the trouble he had with re-adjusting to the civilian world "started to catch up to him"), suggests that his case was particularly fraught.

And yet, while this tragedy is, in ways, a rare outcome, it points to the broader challenges members of the military face after they've retired from their services. More specifically, many veterans organizations are doing significant work to support military veterans, thereby helping bear the burdens of war—a critical and underappreciated responsibility of all Americans. As a result, it's important to interrogate what responsible parties are doing about it—and learning about how to do it well.

Navigating the Transition

While soldiers, on joining the military, are immediately sent to boot camp to become immersed in the military's ethos and approach, there's nothing similar for soldiers as they transition out of the military and back into the civilian world. As Michael Blecker, director of Swords to Plowshares, put it when discussing the Pathway House shooting: "The Department of Defense doesn't spend any time on decompression for these guys, there's not enough treatment—then you have an incident like this that makes everyone think vets are walking time bombs, that we should fear them. But vets more than anything need to be integrated back into their communities, not isolated."

Indeed, the government is struggling to adequately help veterans transition. For example, a 2011 Pew Research Center survey of 1,853 veterans found that, compared to their pre-9/11 peers, nearly double the number of post-9/11 veterans found re-integration difficult, nodding to the particular difficulty of transitioning back into the post-9/11 civilian world. Similarly, in a 2014 poll by the *Washington Post* and the Kaiser Family Foundation, 51 percent of post-9/11 veterans said that the military wasn't doing enough to help them transition. More recently, the Department of Veterans Affairs has come under scrutiny because of a litany of organizational mishaps and shake-ups (the most recent case being the firing of Secretary of Veterans Affairs David Shulkin), as well as questions over incompetent or malicious leadership.

But while it's easy to focus on what's not going well—both in regards to veterans' care and veterans themselves—I'm not suggesting that veterans don't benefit from existing government efforts. For example, in the 2014 poll mentioned above, though a majority of veterans said that the government wasn't doing enough to help with the transition, "almost 60 percent say the government's response is 'excellent' or 'good,'" with "more than eight in 10 saying their physical, mental and emotional needs are being well met." Moreover, as Jim Craig—an Army veteran turned professor—notes in his 2017 essay on post-traumatic growth: "The latest employment numbers show that veterans are actually more employed than their civilian counterparts. Veterans volunteer more hours, vote more often, and give more money to charity than their non-veteran peers. These are clear indications of growth, not decay."

Civil Society's Contributions

Veterans, as a group, generally succeed in re-integrating into the civilian world. However, it's also the case that the government has been unable to provide all the services needed to help many veterans who struggle during the transition. Fortunately, a large ecosystem of organizations, including those like Pathway Home, exists to help fill that gap.

By providing veterans with a new mission—whether by building a career, joining a new community of like-minded people, or recovering from war wounds—these sorts of veterans organizations may help explain why veterans in general are doing well, even though homelessness and, in particular, suicide rates among them are alarmingly high.

Take the mission of using skills learned in the military to forge a new career path. Whether technical knowledge, leadership skills, or traits such as an ability to work on teams and attention to detail, veterans have much to offer employers as a result of their military service. Organizations like American Dream U and the American Legion help by providing mentors to work with transitioning veterans, resources for veterans to navigate benefits such as the GI Bill, and assistance during the job search. Finding a job is a key step in helping resolve four central issues identified by Louis Celli, national director of veterans affairs and rehabilitation at the American Legion: "where to live, what to do for employment, how to access health care, and how to find purpose in post-military life."

In addition to assistance with finding work, many veterans organizations have helped foster a sense of community among veterans. As they transition out of a more tight-knit, insular military community and into one where the military represents less than 1 percent of a population that generally lacks understanding of and interest in the military, being able to develop a sense of belonging and contributing to society is critical to the success of many veterans. In turn, organizations such as Team Rubicon, which unites veterans with first responders after natural disasters, assists veterans "with three things they lose after leaving the military: a purpose, gained through disaster relief; community, built by serving with others; and identity, from recognizing the impact one individual can make."

Lastly, and relatedly, a number of organizations focusing on health have been instrumental in providing assistance to veterans struggling the most during the re-integration process. In this case, "health" is broadly defined. For example, the Wounded Warrior Project "serves veterans and service members who incurred a physical or mental injury, illness, or wound" as a result of their time in the military by providing "free programs and services to address the needs of wounded warriors and fill gaps in government care." Another example of health-focused veterans organization is, of course, Pathway Home, the site of the March shooting. Part of the unique tragedy of the shooting there is that the three women killed dedicated their lives specifically to helping struggling veterans. By offering a tight-knit residential community and regular medical and psychological treatment for 450 veterans since its opening in 2008, Pathway Home has saved many veterans on the verge of hitting rock bottom.

Of course, the organizations listed above represent just the tip of the iceberg of organizations dedicated to supporting veterans (and their families) as they transition from military to civilian life. Moreover, many of these organizations provide far more than career, community, or health services. But this small sample nonetheless demonstrates that fully and successfully re-integrating into the civilian world can require assistance in all aspects of life.

Doing More

Despite all that, however, there's still more that can be done to help veterans during a potentially precarious time. Beyond those organizations whose explicit mission it is to serve military veterans and service members, civilians ought to support veterans and help close the civil-military divide, at least in part by learning more about our military and, in turn, helping to carry the burdens of war.

In a country with an all-volunteer force that represents a tiny fraction of the overall population, it's all too easy to be superficially appreciative while totally ignorant of the military. As Tami Davis Biddle, a professor of national security at the US Army War College, notes: "We ask a very small number of our citizens to carry the full moral burden of the use of state-sanctioned violence to accomplish political aims. Indeed, most Americans have so completely separated themselves from this responsibility that they no longer realize they own it."

It's the duty of an informed citizen, I'd argue, to understand how, where, and why the country is using force overseas. More broadly, developing even a basic knowledge of how the military works and what it does is an important part of renewing a civic community that, in an era of hyper-partisanship and discord, can counteract the identity crisis beleaguering both veterans and non-veterans alike.

The heartbreaking shooting at Pathway Home is an extreme case of a veteran struggling to overcome the difficulties inherent to transitioning out of the military. But, hopefully, this tragedy can inspire the rest of us to support those individuals who have served on our behalf.

"The diagnostic criteria for PTSD, they assert, represent a faulty, outdated construct that has been badly overextended so that it routinely mistakes depression, anxiety, or even normal adjustment for a unique and particularly stubborn ailment."

PTSD Is Being Dangerously Overdiagnosed

David Dobbs

Post-traumatic stress disorder (PTSD) is the modern name for a condition that has always plagued veterans of battle. However, defining and treating the condition has always been difficult. In the following viewpoint, David Dobbs questions the current use of that diagnosis. The author does not claim that PTSD is not real, but that it is being dangerously overdiagnosed, causing some illnesses to be overtreated while others are missed. In the end, Dobbs says, the modern obsession with PTSD may say as much about the public's difficulty dealing with war as that of the veterans. David Dobbs is a journalist who writes features and essays for publications including the Atlantic, *the* New York Times Magazine, National Geographic, *and other publications.*

"The PTSD Trap: Our Overdiagnosis of PTSD in Vets Is Enough to Make You Sick," by David Dobbs, Condé Nast, March 22, 2012. Reprinted by permission.

As you read, consider the following questions:

1. What are the dangers of a misdiagnosis of PTSD, according to the author?
2. What sort of pushback do people get when they suggest overhauling the VA's approach to PTSD, according to this viewpoint?
3. What does the author mean by "recontextualization," and how can that be applied to the public as well as returning war veterans?

In 2006, soon after returning from military service in Ramadi, Iraq, during the bloodiest period of the war, Captain Matt Stevens of the Vermont National Guard began to have a problem with PTSD, or post-traumatic stress disorder. Stevens's problem was not that he had PTSD. It was that he began to have doubts about PTSD: The condition was real, he knew, but as a diagnosis he saw it being dangerously overemphasized.

Stevens led the medics tending an armored brigade of 800 soldiers, and his team patched together GIs and Iraqi citizens almost every day. He saw horrific things. Once home, he had his share, he says, of "nights where I'd wake up and it would be clear I wasn't going to sleep again."

He was not surprised: "I would expect people to have nightmares for a while when they came back." But as he kept track of his unit in the US, he saw troops greeted by both a larger culture and a medical culture, especially in the Department of Veterans Affairs (VA), that seemed reflexively to view bad memories, nightmares and any other sign of distress as an indicator of PTSD.

"Clinicians aren't separating the few who really have PTSD from those who are experiencing things like depression or anxiety or social and reintegration problems, or who are just taking some time getting over it," says Stevens. He worries that many of these men and women are being pulled into a treatment and disability regime that will mire them in a self-fulfilling vision of a brain rewired, a psyche permanently haunted.

Stevens, now a major, and still on reserve duty while he works as a physician's assistant, is far from alone in worrying about the reach of PTSD. Over the last five years or so, a long-simmering academic debate over PTSD's conceptual basis and rate of occurrence has begun to boil over into the practice of trauma psychology and to roil military culture as well. Critiques, originally raised by military historians and a few psychologists, are now being advanced by a broad array of experts, including giants of psychology, psychiatry, diagnosis, and epidemiology such as Columbia's Robert Spitzer and Michael First, who oversaw the last two editions of the American Psychiatric Association's *Diagnostic and Statistical Manual of Mental Disorders*, the *DSM-III* and *DSM-IV*; Paul McHugh, the longtime chair of Johns Hopkins University's psychiatry department; Michigan State University epidemiologist Naomi Breslau; and Harvard University psychologist Richard McNally, a leading authority in the dynamics of memory and trauma, and perhaps the most forceful of the critics. The diagnostic criteria for PTSD, they assert, represent a faulty, outdated construct that has been badly overextended so that it routinely mistakes depression, anxiety, or even normal adjustment for a unique and particularly stubborn ailment.

This quest to scale back the definition of PTSD and its application stands to affect the expenditure of billions of dollars, the diagnostic framework of psychiatry, the effectiveness of a huge treatment and disability infrastructure, and, most important, the mental health and future lives of hundreds of thousands of US combat veterans and other PTSD patients. Standing in the way of reform is conventional wisdom, deep cultural resistance and foundational concepts of trauma psychology. Nevertheless it is time, as Spitzer recently argued, to "save PTSD from itself."

Casting a Wide Net

The overdiagnosis of PTSD, critics say, shows in the numbers, starting with the seminal study of PTSD prevalence, the 1990 National Vietnam Veterans Readjustment Survey. The NVVRS covered more than 1,000 Vietnam veterans in 1988 and reported that 15.4 percent of them had PTSD at that time and 31 percent had suffered it at some point since the war. That 31 percent has been the standard estimate of PTSD incidence among veterans ever since.

In 2006, however, Columbia University epidemiologist Bruce Dohrenwend, hoping to resolve nagging questions about the study, reworked the numbers. When he had culled the poorly documented diagnoses, he found that the 1988 rate was 9 percent, and the lifetime rate just 18 percent.

McNally shares the general admiration for Dohrenwend's careful work. Soon after it was published, however, McNally asserted that Dohrenwend's numbers were still too high because he counted as PTSD cases those veterans with only mild, subdiagnostic symptoms, people rated as "generally functioning pretty well." If you included only those suffering "clinically significant impairment"—the level generally required for diagnosis and insurance compensation in most mental illness—the rates fell yet further, to 5.4 percent at the time of the survey and 11 percent lifetime. It was not 1 in 3 veterans that eventually got PTSD, but 1 in 9—and only 1 in 18 had it at any given time. The NVVRS, in other words, appears to have overstated PTSD rates in Vietnam vets by almost 300 percent.

"PTSD is a real thing, without a doubt," says McNally. "But as a diagnosis, PTSD has become so flabby and overstretched, so much a part of the culture, that we are almost certainly mistaking other problems for PTSD, and thus mistreating them."

The idea that PTSD is overdiagnosed seems to contradict reports of resistance in the military and the VA to recognizing PTSD—denials of PTSD diagnoses and disability benefits, military clinicians discharging soldiers instead of treating them, and a disturbing increase in suicides among veterans of the Middle East wars. Yet the two trends are consistent. The VA's PTSD caseload has more than doubled since 2000, mostly owing to newly diagnosed Vietnam veterans. The poor and erratic response to current soldiers and recent vets, with some being pulled in quickly to PTSD treatments and others discouraged or denied, may be the panicked stumbling of an overloaded system.

Overhauling both the diagnosis and the VA's care system, say critics, will ensure better care for genuine PTSD patients as well as those being misdiagnosed. But the would-be reformers face fierce opposition. "This argument," McNally notes, "tends to really piss some people off." Veterans send him threatening emails. Colleagues accuse him of dishonoring veterans, dismissing suffering, discounting the costs of war. Dean Kilpatrick, a University of South Carolina traumatologist who is president of the International Society for Traumatic Stress Studies (ISTSS), once essentially called McNally a liar.

A Problematic Diagnosis

The most recent Diagnostic and Statistical Manual (*DSM-IV*) defines PTSD as the presence of three symptom clusters—reexperiencing via nightmares or flashbacks; numbing or withdrawal; and hyperarousal, evident in irritability, insomnia, aggression, or poor concentration—that arise in response to a life-threatening event.

Both halves of this definition are suspect. To start with, the link to a traumatic event, which makes PTSD almost unique among complex psychiatric diagnoses in being defined by an external cause, also makes it uniquely problematic, for the tie is really to the memory of an event. When PTSD was first added to the *DSM-III* in 1980, traumatic memories were considered reasonably faithful recordings of actual events. But as research since then has repeatedly shown, memory is spectacularly unreliable and extraordinarily malleable. We routinely add or subtract people, details, settings, and actions to our memories. We conflate, invent, and edit.

In one study by Washington University memory researcher Elizabeth Loftus, one out of four adults who were told they were lost in a shopping mall as children came to believe it. Some insisted the event happened even after the ruse was exposed. Bounteous research since then has confirmed that such false memories are common.

Soldiers enjoy no immunity from this tendency. A 1990s study at the New Haven, Connecticut VA hospital asked 59 Gulf War veterans about their war experiences a month after their return and again two years later. The researchers asked about 19 specific types of potentially traumatic events, such as witnessing deaths, losing friends, and seeing people disfigured. Two years out, 70 percent of the veterans reported at least one traumatic event they had not mentioned a month after returning, and 24 percent reported at least three such events for the first time. And the veterans recounting the most "new memories" also reported the most PTSD symptoms.

To McNally, such results suggest that some veterans experiencing "late-onset" PTSD may be attributing symptoms of depression, anxiety, or other subtle disorders to a memory that has been elaborated and given new significance—or even unconsciously (and innocently) fabricated.

"This has nothing to do with gaming or working the system or consciously looking for sympathy," he says. "We all do this: We cast our lives in terms of narratives that help us understand them. A vet who's having a difficult life may remember a trauma, which may or may not have actually traumatized him, and everything makes sense."

To make PTSD diagnosis more rigorous, some have suggested that blood chemistry, brain imaging or other tests might be able to detect physiological signatures of PTSD. Studies of stress hormones in groups of PTSD patients show differences from normal subjects, but the overlap between the normal and the PTSD groups is huge, making individual profiles useless for diagnostics. Brain imaging has similar limitations, with the abnormal dynamics in PTSD heavily overlapping those of depression and anxiety.

With memory unreliable and biological markers elusive, diagnosis depends on clinical symptoms. But as a 2007 study showed starkly, PTSD's symptom profile is as slippery as the would-be biomarkers. Alexander Bodkin, a psychiatrist at Harvard's McLean Hospital, screened 90 clinically depressed patients separately for PTSD symptoms and for trauma, then compared the results. First he and a colleague used a standardized PTSD screening interview to assess PTSD symptoms. Then two other PTSD diagnosticians, ignorant of the symptom reports, used a standard interview to see which patients had ever experienced trauma fitting *DSM-IV* criteria.

If PTSD arose from trauma, the patients with PTSD symptoms should have histories of trauma, and those with trauma should show more PTSD. It was not so. While the symptom screens rated 70 of the 90 patients PTSD-positive, the trauma screens found only 54 who had suffered trauma; the diagnosed PTSD "cases" outnumbered those who had experienced traumatic events. Things got worse when Bodkin compared the diagnoses one-on-one. If PTSD required trauma, then the 54 trauma-exposed patients should account for most of the 70 PTSD-positive patients. But the PTSD-symptomatic patients were equally distributed among the trauma-positive and the trauma-negative groups. The PTSD rate had zero relation to the trauma rate. It was, Bodkin observed, "a scientifically unacceptable situation."

More practically, as McNally points out, "To give the best treatment, you have to have the right diagnosis."

The most effective treatment for patients whose symptoms arose from trauma is exposure-based cognitive behavioral therapy (CBT), which concentrates on altering the response to a specific traumatic memory by repeated, controlled exposure to it. "And it works," says McNally. "If someone with genuine PTSD goes to the people who do this really well, they have a good chance of getting better." CBT for depression, in contrast, teaches the patient to recognize dysfunctional loops of thought and emotion and develop new responses to normal, present-day events. "If a depressed person takes on a PTSD interpretation of their troubles and gets exposure-based CBT, you're going to miss the boat," says McNally. "You're going to spend your time chasing this memory down instead of dealing with the way the patient misinterprets present events."

To complicate the matter, recent studies showing that traumatic brain injuries from bomb blasts, common among solders in Iraq, produce symptoms almost indistinguishable from PTSD. One more overlapping symptom set.

"The overlap issue worries me tremendously," says Gerald Rosen, a University of Washington psychiatrist who has worked extensively with PTSD patients. "We have to ask how we got here. We have to ask ourselves, 'What do we gain by having this diagnosis?'"

Disabling Conditions

Rosen is thinking of clinicians when he asks about gain. But what does a veteran gain with a PTSD diagnosis? One would hope, of course, that it grants access to effective treatment and support. This is not happening. In civilian populations, two-thirds of PTSD patients respond to treatment. But as psychologist Chris Frueh, who researched and treated PTSD for the VA from the early 1990s until 2006, notes, "In the two largest VA studies of combat veterans, neither showed a treatment effect. Vets getting PTSD treatment from the VA are no more likely to get better than they would on their own."

The reason, says Frueh, is the collision of the PTSD construct's vagaries with the VA's disability system, in which every benefit seems structured to discourage recovery.

The first benefit is healthcare. PTSD is by far the easiest mental health diagnosis to have declared "service-connected," a designation that often means the difference between little or no care and broad, lasting health coverage. Service connection also makes a vet eligible for monthly disability payments of up to $4,000. That link may explain why most veterans getting PTSD treatment from the VA report worsening symptoms until they are designated 100 percent disabled—at which point their use of VA mental health services drops by 82 percent. It may also help to explain why, although the risk of PTSD from a traumatic event drops as time passes, the number of Vietnam veterans applying for PTSD disability almost doubled between 1999 and 2004, driving total PTSD disability payments to more than $4 billion annually. Perhaps most disastrously, these payments continue only if you're sick. For unlike a vet who has lost a leg, a vet with PTSD loses disability benefits as soon as he recovers or starts working. The entire system seems designed to encourage chronic disability.

"In the several years I spent in VA PTSD clinics," says Frueh, "I can't think of a single PTSD patient who left treatment because he got better. But the problem is not the veterans. The problem is that the VA's disability system, which is 60 years old now, ignores all the intervening research we have on resilience, on the power of expectancy and the effects of incentives and disincentives. Sometimes I think they should just blow it up and start over." But with what?

Richard Bryant, an Australian PTSD researcher and clinician, suggests a disability system more like that Down Under. An Australian soldier injured in combat receives a lifelong "noneconomic" disability payment of $300 to $1,200 monthly. If the injury keeps her from working, she also gets an "incapacity" payment, as well as job training and help finding work. Finally—a crucial feature—she retains all these benefits for two years once she goes back to work. After that, her incapacity payments taper to zero over five years. But her noneconomic payments—a sort of financial Purple Heart—continue forever. And like all Australians, she gets free lifetime health care.

Australian vets come home to an utterly different support system from ours: Theirs is a scaffold they can climb. Ours is a low-hanging "safety net" liable to trap anyone who falls in.

Two Ways to Carry a Rifle

When a soldier comes home, he must try to reconcile his war experience with the person he was beforehand and the society and family he returns to. He must engage in what psychologist Rachel Yehuda, who researches PTSD at the Bronx VA hospital, calls "recontextualization"—the process of integrating trauma into normal experience. It is what we all do, on a smaller scale, when we suffer breakups, job losses, the deaths of loved ones. Initially the event seems an impossible aberration. Then slowly we accept the trauma as part of the complex context that is life.

Matt Stevens recognizes this can take time. Even after a year home, the war still occupies his dreams. Sometimes, for instance, he dreams that he is doing something completely normal—while carrying his combat rifle.

"One night I dreamt I was birdwatching with my wife. When we saw a bird, she would lift her binoculars, and I would lift my rifle and watch the bird through the scope. No thought of shooting it. Just how I looked at the birds."

It would be easy to read Stevens's dream as a symptom of PTSD, expressing fear, hypervigilance, and avoidance. Yet the dream can also be seen as demonstrating his success in recontextualizing his experience. He is reconciling the man who once used a gun with the man who no longer does.

Saving PTSD from itself, say Spitzer, McNally, Frueh, and other critics, will require a similar shift—seeing most post-combat distress not as a disorder but as part of normal, if painful, healing. This will involve, for starters, revising the PTSD diagnosis construct—presently under review for the new *DSM-V* due to be published in 2012—so it accounts for the unreliability of memory and better distinguishes depression, anxiety, and phobia from true PTSD. Mental-health evaluations need similar revisions so they can detect genuine cases without leading patients to impose trauma narratives on other mental-health problems. Finally, Congress should replace the VA's disability regime with an evidence-based system that removes disincentives to recovery—and even go the extra mile and give all combat veterans, injured or not, lifetime healthcare.

These changes will be hard to sell in a culture that resists any suggestion that PTSD is not a common, even inevitable, consequence of combat. Mistaking its horror for its prevalence, people assume PTSD is epidemic, ignoring all evidence to the contrary.

The biggest longitudinal study of soldiers returning from Iraq and Afghanistan, led by VA researcher Charles Milliken and published in 2007, seemed to confirm that we should expect a high incidence of PTSD. It surveyed combat troops immediately on return from deployment and again about 6 months later and found around 20 percent symptomatically "at risk" of PTSD. But of those reporting symptoms in the first survey, half had improved by the second survey, and many who first claimed few or no symptoms later reported serious symptoms. How many of the early "symptoms" were just normal adjustment? How many of the later symptoms were the imposition of a trauma narrative onto other problems? Matt Stevens, for one, is certain these screens are mistaking many going through normal adjustment as dangerously at risk of PTSD. Even he, although functioning fine at work, home, and in society, scored positive in both surveys; he is, in other words, one of the 20 percent "at risk." Finally, and weirdly, both screens missed about 75 percent of those who actually sought counseling—a finding that raises further doubts about the screens' accuracy. Yet this study received prominent media coverage emphasizing that PTSD rates were probably being badly undercounted.

A few months later, another study—the first to track large numbers of soldiers through the war—provided a clearer and more consistent picture. Led by US Navy researcher Tyler Smith and published in the *British Medical Journal*, the study monitored mental health and combat exposure in 50,000 US soldiers from 2001 to 2006. The researchers took particular care to tie symptoms to types of combat exposure and demographic factors. Among the 20,000 troops who went to Iraq, 4.3 percent developed diagnosis-level symptoms of PTSD. The rate ran about 8 percent in those with combat exposure and 2 percent in those not exposed.

These numbers are about a quarter of the rates Milliken found. But they're a close match to PTSD rates seen in British Iraq War vets and to rates McNally calculated for Vietnam veterans. The contrast to the Milliken study, along with the consistency with British rates and with McNally's NVVRS calculation, should have made the Smith study big news. Yet the media, the VA, and the trauma psychology community almost completely ignored the study. "The silence," McNally wryly noted, "was deafening."

This silence may be merely a matter of good news going unremarked. Yet it supports McNally's contention that we have a cultural obsession with trauma. The selective attention supports too the assertion by military historian and PTSD critic Ben Shephard that American society itself gained something from the creation of the PTSD diagnosis in the late 1970s: a vision of war's costs that transforms our soldiers from perpetrators to victims—and in doing so, absolves the rest of us for sending them, for we too were victimized, fooled into supporting a war we later regretted. It's good that we feel soldiers' pain. But to impose on a distressed soldier the notion that his memories are inescapable, that he lacks the strength to incorporate his past into his future, is to highlight our moral sensitivity at the soldier's expense.

PTSD exists. Where it exists we must treat it. But our cultural obsession with PTSD has magnified and replicated and institutionalized PTSD until it has finally become the thing itself—a prolonged failure to contextualize and accept our own collective aggression. It may be our own postwar neurosis.

> *"Performance scores reveal that VA hospitals actually exceed non-VA facilities in several key areas of both clinical and quality care."*

The VA Health Care System Performs as Well as or Better than Non-VA Systems

Rachel Grande

While recognizing the efforts of various organizations, the previous viewpoint focused on the role that individual citizens can play in helping returning veterans adjust to civilian life. In the following viewpoint, Rachel Grande takes a close look at the US Department of Veterans Affairs (VA) health care system. The author acknowledges recent scandals and criticism of the agency. However, she also presents data that argues the agency provides higher quality services than non-VA health care facilities. Rachel Grande is a writer specializing in health care content marketing.

"The VA Healthcare System: A Broken System with Superior Quality," Rachel Grande, Definitive Healthcare, April 24, 2017. Reprinted by permission.

As you read, consider the following questions:

1. How are patients at VA hospitals and clinics different from patients at other facilities? Why does this matter when evaluating data about outcomes?
2. Why are VA health care facilities subject to more oversight than non-VA facilities?
3. What does the author point out about the difference between patient satisfaction scores and clinical quality ratings?

V eterans' benefit and assistance agencies have a long history in the United States, with roots tracing all the way back to 1636 and the pilgrims at Plymouth Colony. However, the Veterans Administration (VA)—or the US Department of Veterans Affairs, as we now know it—was not formally established by former President Herbert Hoover until July 1930.

The long-standing goal of these agencies has always been to provide crucial medical care, dental care, rehabilitation, disability compensation, and employment benefits to those who have risked their lives in defense of the country. Within the past 40 years or so, though, the VA healthcare system has weathered criticism for its treatment of veteran patients.

A 2014 scandal, for instance, indicated that VA hospitals may have falsified records to cover up long patient wait times. Evidence of a "secret wait list" revealed that at least 1,700 veterans waited an average of 115 days, or about four months, to see their primary care provider. At one Phoenix, Arizona VA hospital, investigation confirmed that as many as 40 veterans died while on the wait list.

Despite this, performance scores reveal that VA hospitals actually exceed non-VA facilities in several key areas of both clinical and quality care.

In 2010, the VA healthcare system began collaborating with the Centers for Medicare and Medicaid Services (CMS) to regularly publish their clinical and quality scores on the CMS Hospital

Compare website—allowing consumers to readily access this information. Before this time, VA hospital ratings had been kept private. This is reportedly due to fear that bad scores might unfairly tarnish individual hospitals.

In this blog, we've highlighted several key areas in which VA hospitals closely compete with non-VA facilities or, in some cases, outperform them.

Lower Inpatient Mortality Rates at VA Hospitals

The VA healthcare system provides care to more than 9 million enrollees at over 1,200 different healthcare facilities—including 170 VA hospitals and just over 1,000 VA-associated outpatient clinics.

According to Definitive Healthcare data, these 170 VA hospitals consistently outperform non-VA hospitals in average mortality rate for heart attack, heart failure, and pneumonia.

Fig 1. 30-day readmission and mortality rates at VA hospitals vs. non-VA hospitals

MEASURE	READMISSION RATE VA HOSPITALS	READMISSION RATE NON-VA HOSPITALS	MORTALITY RATE VA HOSPITALS	MORTALITY RATE NON-VA HOSPITALS
Heart Attack	17.24	15.7	12.09	12.84
Heart Failure	22.94	21.64	9.62	11.63
Pneumonia	17.47	16.63	13.02	15.78
COPD	15	19.5	N/A	8.54

Fig 1. Data table compares average 30-day readmission and mortality rates as percentages at 168 VA hospitals and 7,044 non-VA hospitals. Data is sourced from the CMS Quality Metrics Update January 2020, and accessed on the Definitive Healthcare Hospitals & IDNs database. Accessed March 2020.

The data table Fig. 1 indicates that VA hospitals report anywhere from 0.75 to 2.76 percent lower mortality rates across all three major condition measures tracked by CMS. Though the mortality rate is markedly lower among veterans' hospitals, these facilities have recently reported higher 30-day readmission rates than non-VA facilities in all reporting areas except for one: chronic obstructive pulmonary disease (COPD).

While average readmission rates at VA hospitals may be consistently higher than those at non-VA hospitals, it's worth noting that these rates are, on average, only about 1.5 percent greater than other facilities.

Improved Patient Safety Indicators at VA Hospitals

The Agency for Healthcare Research and Quality (AHRQ) is a US Department of Health and Human Services agency dedicated to providing evidence that will make the US healthcare system safer, more affordable, and of a higher quality. One of the many ways in which the AHRQ achieves this goal is by tracking patient safety indicators related to certain surgical or other procedural complications.

There are 26 different patient safety indicators, and all hospitals are awarded a score for each of these complications based on how often adult patients were treated for these serious, potentially preventable problems. The resulting score is a composite complication rate per every 1,000 patients.

Definitive Healthcare data reveals that VA hospitals perform better than non-VA hospitals across four of the most frequently reported surgical complications (Fig 2).

Fig 2. Serious complication rate at VA hospitals vs. non-VA hospitals

SERIOUS COMPLICATION MEASURE	VA HOSPITALS (RATE PER 1000 DISCHARGES)	NON-VA HOSPITALS (RATE PER 1000 DISCHARGES)
Collapsed lung due to medical treatment	0.038	0.27
A wound that splits open after surgery on the abdomen	0.90	0.95
Accidental puncture or laceration from medical treatment	0.82	1.29

Fig 2. Data table compares average serious complication rates at 168 VA hospitals and 7,044 non-VA hospitals. Patient safety indicator data sourced from the AHRQ as of January 2020, and accessed on the Definitive Healthcare Hospitals and IDNs database. Accessed March 2020.

The VA Has Three Main Problems

President Donald Trump dismissed Secretary of Veterans Affairs David J. Shulkin on March 28 because he resisted plans to privatize VA medical services, according to Shulkin.

If confirmed, Shulkin will be replaced by Adm. Ronny Jackson, the White House physician who has no experience administering a large organization like the VA and is best known for his fulsome report on Trump's health following an annual physical in January 2018.

The VA has long been in crisis. Nevertheless, it has pioneered evidence-based medicine and, overall, gets better outcomes at lower costs than many private health care providers.

As someone who has studied government budgets and the organization of government agencies, I believe Admiral Jackson, like his predecessor, will have to address three major problems if the VA is to be effective in meeting the needs of the millions of veterans who depend on it for their care.

First, the VA is funded much less generously than private medical providers. That means VA doctors earn substantially less than other physicians, making it hard to fill vacancies.

Second, the VA has no control over the number or location of veterans who gain the right to medical care through their military

Low mortality rates and few post-surgical complications are two evidence-based claims that support quality of care at VA hospitals. Several other factors may also play a role in impacting this quality difference.

In 2015, for instance, the Veterans Administration launched a Diffusion of Excellence program designed to "identify, test, and diffuse" improved quality measures and clinical best practices across the VA healthcare system. Later, in 2017, the administration announced plans to introduce a high-tech healthcare improvement center aimed at specifically addressing facilities with lower performance.

In addition, the VA's status as a federal administration means that it is subjected to more oversight and scrutiny than other service. ... The wars in Afghanistan and Iraq made 4 million additional veterans eligible for VA medical services. Dramatic advances in saving the lives of wounded soldiers means there are more severely disabled veterans needing complex care. Growing understanding of the psychological effects of combat has led to a dramatic increase in the number of veterans who apply for and can benefit from psychological treatment.

Finally, many conservatives and for-profit health providers in search of new customers want to convert the VA into a conduit for government money to buy private insurance or care for veterans. Private care is more expensive and generally of lower care than what the VA now provides. Thus, to increase the use of private facilities will disrupt the continuity of care that is the basis for much of the VA's lower costs and better outcomes. Funds diverted to pay for private care will rob the VA of resources needed to hire more doctors and nurses or to build facilities where they are needed.

President Trump said he fired Shulkin to facilitate further privatization. Veterans' organizations and members of Congress from both parties oppose privatizing because of the deleterious budgetary and health effects they say it would have.

"These Are the VA's 3 Main Problems—Leadership Isn't One of Them," by Richard Lachmann, The Conversation, March 30, 2018.

privately-owned healthcare systems might be. With its performance data now readily accessible to researchers and consumers alike, public pressure has increasingly become a significant motivator in these quality improvement initiatives.

Competitive Patient Satisfaction Scores at VA Hospitals

Despite their relatively high clinical performance, VA hospitals report mixed scores in patient satisfaction surveys.

The Hospital Consumer Assessment of Healthcare Providers and Systems (HCAHPS) is a publicly reported, qualitative evaluation of hospital performance randomly administered to patients within six weeks of hospital discharge. The assessment measures a total of 27 different aspects of hospital care, conduct, and quality in areas related to the patient experience.

According to Definitive Healthcare data, VA hospitals tend to report lower HCAHPS scores than non-VA hospitals across both individual quality measures and overall hospital performance.

Fig 3. HCAHPS patient satisfaction scores at VA hospitals vs. non-VA hospitals

HCAHPS MEASURE	VA HOSPITALS	NON-VA HOSPITALS
Strongly agree that doctors always communicated well	80	81.32
Strongly agree that nurses always communicated well	79	80.60
Strongly agree that staff always explained medicines	67	65.69
Strongly agree that they received help as soon as they wanted	68	69.65
Strongly agree that the room was always quiet at night	59	61.50
Strongly agree that the room and bathroom were always clean	72	75.28
Strongly agree that they were given information about what to do during at-home recovery	86	87.08
Strongly agree that they understood discharge instructions	57	53.08
Rated the hospital a 9 or 10 on a 0 to 10 scale	72	72.72
Would definitely recommend the hospital	71	71.90

Data table compares average response rates on the HCAHPS Patient Satisfaction Survey across 168 VA hospitals and 7,044 non-VA hospitals. HCAHPS data is sourced from the CMS Quality Metrics Update January 2020, and accessed on the Definitive Healthcare Hospitals & IDNs database. Accessed March 2020.

Based on the above table (Fig. 3), VA hospitals report the greatest negative difference in quality performance within the following two areas:

- Patients strongly agree that the room and bathroom were always clean, and
- Patients strongly agree that the area around the room was always quiet at night

It is worth pointing out, however, that neither of these two performance areas are directly related to clinical quality at VA hospitals. In fact, VA hospitals compete closely with non-VA facilities in most other HCAHPS performance measures listed above.

In two cases, VA hospitals actually perform better than non-VA hospitals in terms of clearly communicating medications and helping patients to understand their post-discharge instructions.

Given the subjectivity of the HCAHPS patient satisfaction survey, there are a multitude of other factors impacting hospital scores that might be outside of their control. Noise complaints and cleanliness, for instance, could have more to do with where the hospital is located—as in, a densely-populated urban area—or how old a facility might be. Due to funding restrictions, many VA hospitals have seen little or no facility improvements since they were first constructed.

These things, combined with an always-present staffing shortage at both VA and non-VA hospitals, add nuance to problems that patient insights might otherwise highlight.

> *"Despite the startup issues, which have been glossed over in public discussion of the project, the White House continues to make the overhaul of the military and VA medical records a centerpiece of its government reform efforts."*

The VA Faces Trouble When Integrating the Military's New Electronic Records System

Arthur Allen

According to data cited in the previous viewpoint, the VA health care system provides high-quality clinical care. In the following viewpoint, however, Arthur Allen argues that a disastrous upgrade to digital records of the military health care system bodes poorly for the VA system, when it, too, makes the transition to electronic medical records, posing potentially life-threatening risks to veterans. Arthur Allen is a health care reporter for Politico Pro.

"We Took a Broken System and Just Broke It Completely," by Arthur Allen, Politico, March 8, 2018. Reprinted by permission.

As you read, consider the following questions:

1. What are some of the dangers of a digitized medical records system that doesn't function properly?
2. How did the administration mislead the public about the rollout of the electronic health care records system and its merger with the VA's system?
3. What are some of the reasons for the disastrous rollout of the new electronic system?

President Donald Trump last year hailed a multibillion-dollar initiative to create a seamless digital health system for active duty military and the VA that he said would deliver "faster, better, and far better quality care."

But the military's $4.3 billion Cerner medical record system has utterly failed to achieve those goals at the first hospitals that went online. Instead, technical glitches and poor training have caused dangerous errors and reduced the number of patients who can be treated, according to interviews with more than 25 military and Veterans Affairs health IT specialists and doctors, including six who work at the four Pacific Northwest military medical facilities that rolled out the software over the past year.

Four physicians at Naval Station Bremerton, in the Puget Sound, one of the first hospitals to go online, described an atmosphere so stressful that some clinicians quit because they were terrified they would hurt patients, or even kill them. Prescription requests came out wrong at the pharmacy. Physician referrals failed to go through to specialists. Physicians were unsure how to do basic things such as request lab reports. Doctors complained it could take 10 minutes to get into the system, which then frequently kicked them out. The military's ponderous cybersecurity system was largely to blame, but doctors were frustrated contractors hadn't figured out a way to work around the problems, as they had with the previous electronic record system.

"We took a broken system and just broke it completely," said one doctor, who like most of those interviewed requested anonymity because they lacked military authorization to speak about the project.

Patient Safety Reports—required whenever a life- or limb-threatening medical error is discovered—were "being filed almost every day" in the first few months, said another physician at Bremerton. One report dealt with a patient admitted with a critical heart ailment who later died after getting the wrong treatment, partly because of tests that were sent to another military hospital and lost. The role of Cerner's software in the death is unclear since it is often difficult to pinpoint the specific cause of errors in complex medical systems.

These and other problems, particularly concerns about the VA's ability to share records with civilian health systems, contributed to VA Secretary David Shulkin's decision in December to delay signing a $10 billion contract to install Cerner at the VA, which would be the largest electronic health record job in history. When done, the project would cover 19 million people in the military and VA systems.

Despite the startup issues, which have been glossed over in public discussion of the project, the White House continues to make the overhaul of the military and VA medical records a centerpiece of its government reform efforts.

"This was a huge win for our service," Jared Kushner told a health IT conference in Las Vegas on Tuesday, referring to Shulkin's decision last spring to use Cerner following consultations with Kushner's office. "The president wants to make interoperable health records available for all Americans."

But Kushner's comments gave the impression the military had already created an electronic record system, and was just waiting for the VA to connect to it. In fact, the military's MHS Genesis project, which started rolling out in February 2017, is still in the early stages, with completion scheduled for 2022.

And the tough experiences described by doctors and others suggest a thorny path ahead.

Bob Marshall, a health IT specialist at Madigan Army Medical Center, another early rollout site, blamed the poor start partly on the Pentagon acquisition office's inexperience with civilian record systems and the lack of a "sandbox" where clinicians could perfect the system before it was turned on.

A digital health system must be configured properly before it goes live, said Marshall, who has broad experience in civilian and military IT work. That did not happen in this rollout, he said.

"The bottom line is ... the Cerner user build is immature and needs to be brought up to a functional level," he said. "There were some expectations at higher levels that this ... was an out-of-the-box solution that would work perfectly, but it didn't."

Officials from Cerner and Leidos, the lead contractor on the project, acknowledge startup difficulties but said they're temporary. They said they are making fixes and physicians will get used to other changes. They note that Fairchild Air Force Base near Spokane, Washington, which has a small clinic that went live with the system in February 2017, recently received an industry rating indicating it is making good use of it.

While neither company would comment on safety incidents, Cerner General Manager Travis Dalton said the system overall was making medicine safer.

In the first year, he said, the new computer system issued thousands of meaningful alerts that helped clinicians avoid bad decisions, including a suicide risk alert that has been added to about 100 patient charts.

"I Can't Log Vital Signs or Charts"

Efficiency promises notwithstanding, the new system has resulted in significant slowdowns so far, said physicians at the two hospitals that went live with MHS Genesis in September and October, respectively.

At Bremerton, the system is so cumbersome and confusing that doctors who saw 18 to 20 patients a day now see 12 or 14, they said. When Navy Secretary Richard Spencer came to visit in November, it took staff five minutes to get into the Cerner program. Cerner and military officials declined to comment on the reported incident.

"I'm sitting in front of someone, and the [patient is] launching into their problems, and I can't even open a screen to write them down," said one physician. "I can't log vital signs or charts. I can't write orders in. I have patients I've seen for 12 years, but their data has not migrated over. So I have to log into the old system. Each time, it takes five or 10 minutes to log on. I'm data mining, trying to build a record, address the current problem, find the pitfalls."

At times clinicians could not obtain a patient's latest laboratory results in the system. "You're adjusting medications based on what you think is there," the physician said.

Some staff members have started taking anti-depressants to deal with stress and grief, another doctor said. "The people I work with come to work every day wanting to do a good job, and it doesn't feel good not to."

Defenders of the project said glitches are to be expected.

They note that the military's implementation was complicated by the fact that it was simultaneously upgrading telecommunications hardware at the bases and also moving the medical services of the Navy, Air Force and Army under a single Defense Health Agency command.

After clinician complaints reached a critical mass in December, the military and its partners began an eight- to 10-week "stabilization" period, with experts flown in from Washington and Kansas City, Cerner's home base, to iron out problems. In the process, they are laying down a blueprint to roll out the system at bases in the rest of the country, said Stacy Cummings, who oversees the modernization for the Defense Department.

Cummings said some changes had been made in response to safety red flags. For example, doctors noticed that time-zone differences in the software might be affecting the timing of newborn liver function tests, which are supposed to be performed within a narrow window. That problem was quickly fixed, she said.

"Nobody Is Saying, 'You Got to Turn This Off'"

The expert repair team sent out to Madigan in mid-January will remain through March, making some immediate patches while major software redesigns are performed at Cerner headquarters through May, Cummings said. Senior officials could sign off on the Pacific Northwest rollout—known as the initial operating capability, or IOC—in the summer. If that happens, the military will start implementing the next wave, with medical facilities from San Diego to Alaska going live in 2019.

In an interview, leaders of the project from Leidos, the lead contractor, Cerner and Accenture, another big subcontractor, said medical staff everywhere often react with frustration and anger to new digital record systems. But the executives acknowledged problems and said they were working together to fix them.

Cerner software templates that matched particular types of clinicians with access to certain information and capacities were mismatched with the military's system, said Jerry Hogge, deputy group president of Leidos Health Solutions.

"We found we had to refine how roles and training were aligned, and the workflows we designed needed to be redesigned," he said. "But that's why we wanted to have the IOC, to shake all those things out."

"The most challenging part of any of these deployments is the change process," Hogge added. "The human nature part of learning something new."

"They [physicians] say they want things better, but nobody is saying, 'You got to turn this off,'" said David Norley, Cummings' senior aide.

Cummings acknowledged that clinicians should have been taught more about the new processes required of them before the system went live. Officials are also working to make it easier for physicians to get into the system, but the military's cybersecurity precautions mean it will never be as painless as in civilian medicine, she said.

In the six weeks since the review started, there have been changes for the better, at least at Madigan, the largest of the four facilities, said Marshall, who was chief medical information officer there before retiring three years ago. He returned in part to help with the implementation.

At Madigan, the system now shows physicians a single menu where they can view patients in outpatient, inpatient or maternity care, he said. Broken scroll bars that made it hard to order drugs or lab tests have been fixed.

"That doesn't sound like much, but it's extra seconds per patient," Marshall said.

Physicians at Madigan and Bremerton said the software works well in their emergency rooms.

Madigan is the only of the four bases to have a team of medical IT experts who can speak the same language as both computer engineers and doctors.

Bigger Challenges Ahead for VA

The military's troubles have offered the VA an opportunity to examine potential bugs before launching its Cerner project, which is expected to take 10 years.

"We've learned from where the Department of Defense would have chosen to go if they had the information we have now, and we think we're working on a much better, stronger contract that will avoid some of the problems we've seen in [the MHS Genesis] implementation," Shulkin told reporters last week.

Shulkin continues to say that when the problems are resolved and the system built, it will transform how information is shared among doctors and hospitals across the US health care system. The VA eventually will get 30 percent more capability than the military has, he said.

However, MHS Genesis' troubles alarm some VA officials, who note their health care system is vastly larger and more complex than the one run by the military. It also takes care of a generally sicker population, often dependent on records that stretch back decades.

Shulkin's decision to delay the contract won widespread praise, but critics bemoan his decision last year to shutter an internal program to modernize the VA's existing digital record system, known as VistA. Many health IT experts left the agency after cancellation of the program, which involved hundreds of staff and contractors.

Partly due to political strains at the agency, where Shulkin's job appeared at risk, the VA is without senior officials who would make key decisions in the Cerner implementation. There is no chief information officer, for example, and the Veterans Health Administration lacks both a director and a senior IT officer.

"The VA is in kind of a holding pattern," said a mid-level IT director there. "We don't have advocates for some of the things that really need advocacy."

VA spokesman Curt Cashour declined to allow the VA officials leading the Cerner deal to speak with POLITICO, citing the pending contract talks.

But four senior health IT experts who were involved in the internal project told POLITICO that while they understood Shulkin's desire to jettison expensive programs, he might regret the loss of expertise and technology, which they believe could make the Cerner implementation truly transformative.

"We're doing a once-in-a-lifetime replacement of an ... [existing electronic health record system] that's pretty functional—some of our physicians like it better than Epic or Cerner," said a recently retired VA official. "Why replace it with something that's basically the same?"

Two of the VA officials who left the agency expressed concern about whether clinicians will be able to access needed data from patients who are seen in both the Cerner and VA digital systems during the long conversion to Cerner. To achieve this goal will require significant investment, they said.

Shulkin has met with other software vendors and health care systems to discuss solutions that might tie together veteran and active duty records during the long transition to a single platform, according to a close associate.

House Veterans Affairs Chairman Phil Roe (R-Tenn.) recently visited Fairchild Air Force Base—home of the first military clinic rollout—and returned shaking his head. Roe, a retired obstetrician-gynecologist, noted that doctors at the base couldn't easily call up patients' records. The VA may face the same problems, he said.

The $10 billion Cerner contract, Roe noted, "doesn't even include the costs of updating infrastructure to accommodate the new [record system], implementation support or sustaining VistA up until the day it can be turned off."

| "When it works best, the VA is like
concierge care for poor people."

Free Market Zealots Are Trying to Destroy the VA

Suzanne Gordon

It has been pointed out in previous viewpoints that the VA health care system provides better care than most private health care systems. In this viewpoint, an interview in the magazine Jacobin, *Suzanne Gordon argues that despite this documentable success, the system is often the victim of a deliberate and sustained campaign to wreck it in order to justify the privatization of the agency for the profit of corporations rather than the care of veterans. Suzanne Gordon is a journalist and author of several books on veterans' health care.*

As you read, consider the following questions:

1. What is the motivation for creating the misperception that the VA health care system is a disaster, according to this viewpoint?
2. What strategy does the author say that free-market enthusiasts use to destroy public services, such as public housing, education, and now the VA?
3. How is the effectiveness of the VA health system tied to its interconnectedness?

"The Assault on Veterans' Health Care," by Suzanne Gordon, *Jacobin*, November 6, 2018. Reprinted by permission.

V eterans' health care is "horrible, horrible, and unfair" according to Donald Trump. But how true is that? Pretty untrue, judging by the numerous studies the US Department of Veterans Affairs' (VA) health care system performs better than private systems in quality, safety, and effectiveness of treatment.

The VA runs the largest health care system in the US, and the only one that's publicly funded from top to bottom, with not only its own insurance program but its own doctors and hospitals as well. And despite having an older, poorer, and sicker clientele than the general population, the VA is both the most cost-effective health system in the country and boasts the nation's highest rates of patient satisfaction. Its continuing success is a stinging rebuke to the neoliberal axiom that private corporations and capitalist markets can deliver everything society needs, better and more efficiently than tax-funded social programs can.

It comes as no surprise, then, that free market crusaders like the Koch brothers have set out to convince the public that the VA is actually a disaster. They and other billionaires and hard right-wingers want the Trump administration to do to veteran health care what previous administrations have done to public housing and education: bring it to its knees, then denounce it as a failure, then privatize it.

The script is familiar. First, wage a dishonest propaganda campaign against a functioning public program. Then starve the public program of funds through "fiscally responsible" austerity measures. Point to failures caused by underfunding as evidence of the program's irredeemable flaws. Elevate private alternatives as a panacea for the problems caused by deliberate budget cuts, then repeat until the public program has been eroded and largely replaced by a patchwork of nonpublic entities that treat the original public good like a commodity.

Even the rhetorical tricks are well-worn: just as the "school choice" movement has done in promoting the characterization of public education, and just as HUD's "housing choice" vouchers have done in order to shunt poor people into the private rental market rather than build public housing, the term "veteran choice" has been thrown around to describe siphoning patients out of the VA and into the private sector.

In the name of "veteran choice," earlier this month the Senate passed the VA Mission Act, which will (among other changes, some of which are positive) "streamline veterans' access to non-VA community care"—that is, pay tax dollars for them to leave the VA. The reality, says journalist Suzanne Gordon, is that such privatization efforts will ultimately "increase middleman profits, reduce the efficiencies of a fully integrated system, and drastically cut care."

Jacobin spoke with Gordon about the assault on the VA system. She's the author of several books on veterans' health care; her latest is *The Battle for Veterans' Healthcare: Dispatches from the Frontlines of Policy Making and Patient Care.*

How does the VA differ from other health care systems in America?

SG: Perhaps the important distinction is the level of integration in the VA. The VA is the only fully integrated health care system in America. That means that not only can a veteran go from Philadelphia to Stockton, California, and their health records will follow them seamlessly, but also their care is integrated within each facility.

In VA facilities from Boston to San Francisco you have primary care doctors, mental health specialists, dieticians, social workers, oncologists, palliative care physicians, and pharmacists all in one facility. This allows the VA to deliver care in a way that isn't episodic, it's all connected.

Most private sector health care works like this: you go to your pulmonologist, and you go to your endocrinologist, and the two of them don't talk to each other, and they may never even exchange your records. They just send you from referral to referral, and you run around like that.

Because of the lack of communication, you're not getting the best care you possibly can, and sometimes you'll need a specialist who's out of network, so you've hit a dead end. Plus, with the private-sector referral system, there's a huge non-follow up problem. Making appointments is confusing and difficult, and people just don't do it, which worsens their care quality.

By contrast at the VA, here's a typical story. I was watching one veteran in primary care, and he presented signs of a mental health problem. He was taken by the primary care doctor to the psychiatric nurse practitioner down the hall, introduced to them in what's called a "warm hand off," and then was seen by that person in that clinic. It turned out he also needed an orthopedic appointment, so the psychiatric nurse practitioner walked him down to the ortho floor to get him that appointment too.

I knew one Iraq veteran, a thirty-year-old with the body of a sixty-year-old, with about sixteen different health problems. If he had to go around San Francisco to different doctors, as opposed to the San Francisco VA where it's like one-stop shopping, he told me he'd "be in a ditch."

In the VA, they'll take you down to the pharmacists to talk for forty-five minutes about your meds and how they impact your lifestyle and vice versa. And that's unheard-of in the private sector. You can't get this kind of care in the private sector no matter how good your insurance is, because of the design.

When Steve Jobs was dying of pancreatic cancer, he had all these specialists who didn't talk to each other, and his wife had to collect them at his bedside to get them to coordinate care. This is a multi-billionaire, and he couldn't get the kind of integrated health care you get through the VA.

When it works best, the VA is like concierge care for poor people.

Does this integrated model allow the VA to excel at any particular type of care? I've heard it offers pioneering mental health care and addiction treatment.

SG: The VA excels at a lot of things, including basic primary and preventative care. Most primary care doctors in the private sector have the ten-minute visit, because they have patient panels of between 2,100 and 3,400 patients. In the VA, primary care doctors have between 1,100 and 1,300 patients, so the routine visit is thirty minutes.

On top of that, VA doctors are trained to recognize signs of mental health and substance abuse problems, and since they don't have to work on a referral system, the likelihood of getting the patient into treatment is much higher. So, that partly explains why the VA has such good mental health care.

The VA excels in treatment for all kinds of trauma, including sexual trauma and PTSD. But it's more big-picture than that. The VA also has great geriatric care, women's health programs, physical therapy programs, and palliative care and hospice. The VA has blind rehab centers, spinal cord injury centers, a whole network of centers that serves the entire population of veterans.

And they have homeless outreach programs, and training programs to teach police officers how to deal with mental health crises, which disproportionately impact veterans. And they experiment with new models like team-based primary care, where providers share responsibility for a patient. The integrated system really allows the VA to go above and beyond.

In the VA system, everything is connected. So, for example, suicide prevention is umbilically tied to primary care, to behavioral health, and in the case of many vets to audiology. The number one thing that brings vets to the VA is tinnitus or hearing loss, because there's almost no branch of the military where you aren't assaulted by noise. So, you could go to an audiologist as a veteran, which many first-timers do, and you may say something that the doctor recognizes as a sign of suicidality, and intervention would be possible immediately.

Given that we have a notoriously thin welfare state in the US, how did the VA become so robust?

SG: For most of our history, since the American Revolution, we treated veterans very poorly. Then after World War I, and particularly after World War II, we started building more hospitals for veterans and connecting with academic medical centers. But the VA as we know it is actually a slightly later creation than many big public programs.

The VA delivered mostly inpatient care until the 1990s when Bill Clinton's Undersecretary for Health Kenneth Kizer developed this system of outpatient care and patient safety. He and his team really transformed the VA to what we have today.

Bill Clinton supported it—but tellingly, the Clintons' health care plan from the very beginning hinted at a desire for increased privatization and competition. The VA flourished entirely as a result of Kizer and his team.

By the early 2000s, you had *Businessweek* and *Forbes* hailing the VA as a model of care for the rest of the country. George W. Bush didn't like that, of course, because it counters the narrative of "the market is best for everything," so his administration started clamping down on the good news. That continued under Obama, who failed to vigorously defend the VA.

Of course, the Obama administration was in favor of charter schools and pioneered the Affordable Care Act, both of which uphold this faith in the market and accept a certain degree of privatization. The Obama administration never denounced the VA, but they were tight-lipped about its successes. They didn't champion it in the media or before Congress. They allowed its name to be dragged through the mud by people like the Koch brothers, who founded the group Concerned Veterans for America specifically to spread the story that the VA is a failure, which is a story you see more of all the time.

For people interested in spreading the story that the VA is a train wreck, there was a scandal in 2014 that they could point to, right?

SG: In 2014 there was a crisis, which opponents of the VA used as an opportunity to tarnish the image of the program. The VA central office had imposed an unworkable performance metric on VA providers, demanding that they see patients within fourteen days of calling for an appointment. They offered bonuses to people who met this unrealistic metric, and eventually some VA administrators were caught gaming the system and claiming they met the metric when they didn't. A whistleblower in Phoenix blew this up, and allegations emerged that forty patients had died because they were waiting so long for care.

It's important to note that when this scandal happened, the VA was chronically understaffed, which is partially why the metric was so unworkable. There were 34,000 employee vacancies in 2014. In February of that year, Bernie Sanders tried to get funding to staff the VA appropriately and found that it would cost $21 billion, which Congress refused to allocate. Only later that year did it agree to allocate part of those funds, and most of the money ended up being earmarked for outsourced care, not staffing the VA to capacity.

Later, the VA inspector general later found that only six patients had died, and it was unclear whether they died while or because they were waiting for care, an important distinction. But the Right latched onto the original figure and the media ran with it.

The media also neglected to compare the number to the private sector, in which case the story loses its impact. Hundreds of thousands of people die of treatable illnesses in the US every year who would get care if they were in a system like the VA. And tens of thousands more die every year due to preventable medical errors in private-sector hospitals, which prioritize profit over patient safety.

But in discussing the VA's failures, the media fails to make that comparison. In fact, the double standard is just incredible. A few years ago, a Tea Party politician pointed out that the VA was spending taxpayer money on art in hospitals. Mainstream media outlets ran outraged stories, neglecting to mention that the VA art budget is a miniscule fraction of the total budget, and that art has proven uses in healing. And then the *Wall Street Journal* turns around and runs a front-page story praising the Cleveland Clinic for the art it uses in hospitals.

Can you tell me about the suppression of David Shulkin's book?

SG: When he was Undersecretary of Health under Obama, Shulkin edited a book called *Best Care Everywhere*. It's 400 pages long and has over 150 examples of VA innovation and pioneering clinical programs. Shulkin carried over from the Obama administration to the Trump administration, and the book was published last year, in summer of 2017.

But he never mentioned it once publicly. It's perpetually out of stock at the Government Publishing Office. I heard about it from a friend, who had received one at a leadership conference where Shulkin was giving them out very parsimoniously, and when I called the VA public affairs officer, she said she'd never even heard of it.

Of course, it's been suppressed because it contradicts Trump and the Republicans' narrative. But to me this is hardly the most egregious thing. What's worse is that even when studies showing how effective and innovative the VA is are not suppressed, lawmakers and the media don't pay attention.

There are also studies coming out talking about the problems with private-sector health care in dealing with the complex needs of veterans, and those receive no attention or coverage either. If we looked closer at the evidence of VA excellence, we would have a much harder time justifying the privatization of the VA.

We would conclude that the VA needs to be appropriately funded, not dismantled. For example, instead of funding veterans to go to private urgent-care clinics, we need to build more urgent-care capacity in the VA.

Why would a veteran who gets great care through the VA go to a private clinic or hospital anyway?

SG: Maybe there's a hospital closer to them, maybe they've been persuaded by hospital advertising, maybe a combination of the two. The average hospital spends over a million dollars per year on advertising, while the VA spends next to nothing. You can imagine someone who sees an advertisement over and over on the highway that says, "Come to us for your colonoscopy." And when the time comes, maybe they find it inconvenient to go to the VA facility.

Soon we may see hospitals advertising specifically to veterans. There is also a hedge-fund billionaire, Steven Cohen, who is pouring money into nonprofit veterans' clinics over the next five years specifically to make selection of non-VA care more common, presumably because he'd like to open the market and move into it.

The way the VA works makes it vulnerable to this kind of thing, even though it means better care. The VA has specialized transplant facilities—for example, stem-cell transplants are done in Seattle. So, a veteran who lives anywhere would go to Seattle, and the VA would pay for their airfare, for their hotel, even for their family to come. But a veteran might say, as one in Phoenix did recently, "I don't want to go to Seattle, I want my transplant in Phoenix." And he got it, at the cost of a million dollars, and the VA paid. In Seattle, it would've been $150,000.

If you do the math, this outsourcing is going to drain public money and put it right in the private sector's pockets. And the VA is going to have to have all these conversations with these private hospitals and share records with no uniform system, which is going to mess with the integrated care model that makes the VA work so well.

How similar is this to the "school choice movement," or the charterization of public education?

SG: It's exactly like charter schools. You starve the system, then you say that it can't provide good education for children or health care for veterans. Then you create private options that depend on federal money. Then you create a constituency of parents or veterans for those private options, and it becomes a kind of prestige thing, like "I'm not going to those yucky places anymore," which reinforces the idea that there's something flawed about public education or health care.

When underfunding is brought up you blame the unions, you blame the employees for being greedy. You use murky metrics to assess whether a school or facility is performing well, and if it fails you shut it down. If you read Diane Ravitch's book *Reign of Error*, you could substitute the VA for public schools in pretty much every sentence.

To what extent is the VA's success an argument for nationwide single payer, and to what extent does that animate the attacks on it?

SG: Yes, and yes. Ideally, I believe that we should be fighting for Veterans' Care For All, because Medicare is a payer, not a system. The VA is a payer and a system, it pays for care and delivers care. It can do things that Medicare can't do. That's why it can deliver integrated care.

I think that had the Right not succeeded in tarnishing the program's public image, we could be fighting for a national version of the VA right now. Even so, many of the ways in which the VA excels show us that single payer is a step in the right direction.

And yes, I think that the fundamental impetus behind all these attacks is fear of what the VA stands for. Private hospitals can fire patients, but the VA can't, because it stands for helping people who need help, and taking care of everyone.

> *"Critics point to reports of long wait times for care at some VA facilities and difficulties with the existing community care programs as proof of a system in need of dramatic reforms."*

Congressional Leaders Claim the VA Needs Fixing

Leo Shane III

The previous viewpoint mentioned repeated efforts to misrepresent the facts about the VA health system in order to undermine the publicly funded agency. In the following viewpoint, Leo Shane III turns from the point of view of the VA to that of Congress and looks at how this battle is playing out there. The author highlights how politicized the debate over veterans' care has become and presents voices who disagree with the previous viewpoint by claiming that the VA is indeed in trouble. Leo Shane III is a reporter covering Congress, Veterans' Affairs, and the White House for Military Times.

"Brewing Capitol Hill Fight: Is VA Broken or Under Attack?" by Leo Shane III, Sightline Media Group, April 30, 2019. Reprinted by permission.

As you read, consider the following questions:

1. Which member of Congress is used as a launch point for the author's viewpoint?
2. Do you think the "Veterans' Choice" policy is in the best interest of the VA health system and the veterans it serves?
3. How could providing more "choice" to veterans actually reduce the quality of their care?

F reshman Democratic Rep. Alexandria Ocasio-Cortez again this week defended the Veterans Affairs health system as a vital national resource and criticized Republican opponents of twisting her words on VA operations as part of an effort to undermine the system.

"There is a myth that all VAs everywhere are broken," the New York Democrat said during a town hall meeting on Monday. Video of the event was posted online by the Free Beacon.

"The idea that if we can starve our public systems … if we can starve them of budgets and make sure that they can't do their job, then we can say the whole system should be thrown away."

The comments build on others Ocasio-Cortez made at an April 17 event with union groups, warning of an assault on the Department of Veterans Affairs by Republican leaders who want to "privatize" the department.

But political critics insist the comments show a lack of understanding and compassion by the rising progressive star on the problems facing the VA. They point to reports of long wait times for care at some VA facilities and difficulties with the existing community care programs as proof of a system in need of dramatic reforms.

"Problems and inconsistencies like that are the definition of a system that needs fixing," Rep. Phil Roe, R-Tenn., and ranking member of the House Veterans' Affairs Committee, told Fox News last week. "I am baffled as to how Rep. Ocasio-Cortez fails to see that.

"When you don't know anything about anything, you should probably keep your mouth shut or everyone will know you don't know anything."

At the heart of the fight are sweeping changes to outside health care options set to go into effect in early June. President Donald Trump for months has touted the moves (approved by Congress last summer with bipartisan support) as his administration bringing "choice" to veterans for the first time.

The rules as written by VA officials could more than triple the number of veterans eligible for taxpayer-funded care at private-sector clinics. Numerous Democrats, including House Veterans' Affairs Committee Chairman Mark Takano, D-Calif., have expressed concerns the changes will siphon money and attention away from VA facilities, undermining the system.

Mark Takano *@RepMarkTakano*

VA is not broken, and it's not perfect. It provides some of the best veteran care in the country—that's a fact—but red tape and wait times are unacceptable. I'd ask @DrPhilRoe not to tell members to shut their mouth. @AOC represents veterans, just like the rest of us.

8:58 PM - Apr 24, 2019

Roe and Trump officials have defended the moves as necessary to modernize the health care system by making it more responsive to the needs and wants of veterans.

Ocasio-Cortez' entry into the debate has elevated the issue beyond just the veterans community. She has cast the fight as a conflict between conservatives who are set on dismantling public safety nets to the benefit of more expensive private-sector options, and has advocated for expanded government-backed health care for all Americans.

Her office did not respond to requests for comment. At the union event earlier this month, she said supporters of the private-care expansion are "trying to fix the VA for pharmaceutical companies, they are trying to fix the VA for insurance corporations, and, ultimately they are trying to fix the VA for a for-profit healthcare industry that does not put people or veterans first."

Just a few days later, Trump took to Twitter to criticize her comments, saying that VA "is doing great ... but that is only because of the Trump Administration."

Donald J. Trump *@realDonaldTrump*

Rep. Alexandria Ocasio-Cortez is correct, the VA is not broken, it is doing great. But that is only because of the Trump Administration. We got Veterans Choice & Accountability passed. "President Trump deserves a lot of credit." Dan Caldwell, Concerned Veterans of America

12:54 PM - Apr 24, 2019

Both sets of comments drew pushback this week from fellow Democratic Rep. Seth Moulton, a Massachusetts lawmaker who recently entered the presidential race. During an interview on CNN Sunday, the Iraq War veteran said that "the VA is broken" but supported more investment in the system.

"It doesn't mean that we should just dismantle the VA. If you ask veterans, they want to fix the VA," he said. "We don't want the VA to go away, we just want it to work better. And it's not working right now, so don't tell me the system isn't broken."

VA officials, including Secretary Robert Wilkie, have repeatedly dismissed accusations of privatization of core department responsibilities and said the new community care rules will go into effect on June 6, barring congressional intervention.

Periodical and Internet Sources Bibliography

The following articles have been selected to supplement the diverse views presented in this chapter.

Tony Abraham, "The VA Privatization Debate: 5 Things to Know," *Healthcare Dive*, April 11, 2018. https://www.healthcaredive.com /news/the-va-privatization-debate-5-things-to-know/520618/

Janice Hahn, "Veteran Homelessness Is a Travesty; So Is Opposing Solutions to House Them," *Los Angeles Times*, November 15, 2019. https://www.latimes.com/opinion/story/2019-11-15 /veteran-homelessness-janice-hahn

Ruth Igielnik, "Key Findings About America's Military Veterans," Pew Research, November 7, 2019. https://www.pewresearch.org/fact -tank/2019/11/07/key-findings-about-americas-military-veterans/

Sebastian Jilke and Wouter Van Dooren, "The Question No One Is Asking About Privatizing the VA," January 17, 2019. https:// taskandpurpose.com/opinion/why-privatizing-the-va-or-other -essential-health-services-is-a-bad-idea

Kacie Kelly, "There's More Than One Right Way to Treat PTSD in Veterans," Military.com, February 18, 2020. https://www.military .com/daily-news/2020/02/18/theres-more-one-right-way-treat -ptsd-veterans.html

Phil Klay, "Can the Trauma of War Lead to Growth, Despite the Scars?" *New York Times,* July 6, 2020. https://www.nytimes .com/2020/07/06/health/ptsd-war-trauma-growth.html

John Linder, "The Common Sense Argument for Privatizing the VA," *The Hill,* January 3, 2017. https://thehill.com/blogs/pundits-blog /the-administration/312460-the-common-sense-argument-for -privatizing-the-va

Matthew J. Louis, "Why Veterans Need More Than Transition Assistance Programs," *Military Times*, May 12, 2020. https://www .militarytimes.com/education-transition/2020/05/12/why -veterans-need-more-than-transition-assistance-programs/

For Further Discussion

Chapter 1

1. In the first viewpoint in this chapter, the author discusses something he calls the civilian-military disconnect. Do you see this in your community? Do you agree that there is such a disconnect?
2. What are the potential consequences of a society in which there is a distance between the people who fight wars and the people who send them to fight? Who, typically, are the people who send the military to fight wars?
3. The author of the final viewpoint of this chapter makes the case for compulsory national service—not necessarily military service. He argues that the benefits of citizenship should not be given unless some sort of service to country is given in return. Do you agree? Why or why not? How do you think this plan would go over with the majority of Americans?

Chapter 2

1. The author of the first viewpoint in this chapter points out that since the 1950s, the US has spent an increasingly greater percentage of its budget on things like Welfare, Medicare, and Social Security as opposed to the military. Does this seem like a bad thing to you? Why or why not?
2. In viewpoint four, the author says that the power of what he calls "the new military-industrial complex" renders public opposition useless and disregards the lives of soldiers. How do you think these companies and lobbyists have gained so much power? Should they be stopped? If so, how?
3. In the sixth viewpoint in this chapter, the author talks about how defending the nation extends to guarding its strategic interests. What do you think he means by strategic interests

and why might they be harder to define and measure than mere defense?

Chapter 3

1. The viewpoints discussing women in the military often mention the frequent examples of sexual abuse in the armed forces. Does this seem like a valid reason for banning women from combat roles? Why or why not? If not, what do you think is the best way to address this problem?

2. In the viewpoint tracing the history of US policy regarding LGBTQ service members, the author points out that the US military is typically far ahead of the rest of American society in ending prejudice. In what ways is the military different from civilian society, and how might those differences contribute to more enlightened social views?

3. It is often said that a transgender person "identifies" as a gender other than the gender assigned at birth. In the fifth viewpoint in this chapter, the author explains why the word "identifies" is not the best choice. Can you explain why not? Can you think of a better way to phrase it?

Chapter 4

1. Several of the viewpoints in this chapter point out and even cite data about the quality of veterans' health care. Why is it exceptional that the VA system offers better, more cost-effective care than private health systems? How is the VA able to do this?

2. In the fifth viewpoint, the author argues that free-market zealots are deliberately trying to sabotage the VA. What, according to the author, is their motivation for this? Who stands to gain and who to lose?

3. Other viewpoints acknowledge a scandal at the VA involving long wait times to get care. Does hearing about possible sabotage make a difference to the way you view the VA health system?

Organizations to Contact

The editors have compiled the following list of organizations concerned with the issues debated in this book. The descriptions are derived from materials provided by the organizations. All have publications or information available for interested readers. The list was compiled on the date of publication of the present volume; the information provided here may change. Be aware that many organizations take several weeks or longer to respond to inquiries, so allow as much time as possible.

Children of Fallen Patriots Foundation

44900 Prentice Drive
Dulles, VA 20166
(866) 917-2373
email: Contact via website form
website: www.fallenpatriots.org

This organization provides college scholarships and educational counseling to military children who have lost a parent in the line of duty.

Fisher House Foundation

12300 Twinbrook Parkway
Suite 410
Rockville, MD 20852
(888) 294-8560
email: info@fisherhouse.org
website: www.fisherhouse.org

Fisher House provides homes where veterans and their families can stay free of charge while a loved one is in a military or VHA hospital.

Give an Hour

PO Box 5918
Bethesda, MD 20824-5918
email: info@giveanhour.org
website: www.giveanhour.org

Give an Hour coordinates a network of volunteer professionals who provide free mental health care to active duty, National Guard, and Reserve service members, veterans, and families.

Honor Flight Network

4601 North Fairfax Drive, Suite 1200
Arlington, VA 22203
(937) 521-2400
email: tribute@honorflight.org
website: www.honorflight.org

Honor Flight Network transports America's veterans to Washington, DC, where they can visit the memorials honoring those who have served their country.

Hope for the Warriors

8003 Forbes Place, Suite 201
Springfield, VA 22151
(877) 246-7349
email: info@hopeforthewarriors.org
website: www.hopeforthewarriors.org

Hope for the Warriors provides support programs for service members, veterans, and military families. The organization focuses on transition and health and wellness.

Operation Care and Comfort

1702-L Meridian Avenue, #241
San Jose, CA 95125
(408) 832-2929
email: info@occ-usa.org
website: www.occ-usa.org

This organizations coordinates efforts of the public to provide many types of support to veterans and troops currently serving. Citizens can donate time, talent, and money for various projects, such as care packages.

Semper Fi Fund

Box 555193
Camp Pendleton, CA 92055-5193
(760) 725-3680
email: Contact via website form
website: www.semperfifund.org

The Semper Fi Fund provides urgently needed resources and support for members and the families of members of the US military who have been wounded or are critically ill.

Tragedy Assistance Program for Survivors (TAPS)

3033 Wilson Boulevard, Third Floor
Arlington, VA 22201
(202) 588-8277
email: Contact via website form
website: www.taps.org

Through a national peer support network, TAPS provides comfort, care, and resources to those who have lost a military loved one.

United Service Organizations (USO)

PO Box 96860
Washington, DC 20077-7677
(888) 484-3876
email: Contact via website form
website: www.uso.org

Since 1941, the USO has been a leading service organization for members of the US military and their families. It provides a variety of support services at home, and entertainment for deployed troops.

Vietnam Veterans of America

8719 Colesville Road, Suite 100
Silver Spring, MD 20910
(800) 882-1316
email: Contact via website form
website: www.vva.org

VVA advocates for Vietnam veterans through legislation and community support. Its mission is the ensure that Vietnam vets get both the care and the respect they have earned.

Bibliography of Books

Beth Bailey, *America's Army: Making the All-Volunteer Force.* Cambridge, MA: Belknap, 2009.

Rosa Brooks, *How Everything Became War and the Military Became Everything: Tales from the Pentagon.* New York, NY: Simon and Schuster, 2016.

C. J. Chivers, *The Fighters.* New York, NY: Simon and Schuster, 2018.

Paul Dickson and Thomas B. Allen, *The Bonus Army: An American Epic.* Mineola, NY: Dover, 2020.

Diane Carlson Evans, *Healing Wounds: A Vietnam War Combat Nurse's 10-Year Fight to Win Women a Place of Honor in Washington, DC.* New York, NY: Permuted Press, 2020.

Joseph L. Galloway and Marvin J. Wolf, *They Were Soldiers: The Sacrifices and Contributions of Our Vietnam Veterans.* Nashville, TN: Thomas Nelson, 2020.

Kate Germano, with Kelly Kennedy, *Fight Like a Girl: The Truth Behind How Female Marines Are Trained.* Amherst, NY: Prometheus, 2018.

Suzanne Gordon, *Wounds of War: How the VA Delivers Health, Healing, and Hope to the Nation's Veterans.* Ithaca, NY: ILR Press, 2018.

Caroline Johnson, *Jet Girl: My Life in War, Peace, and the Cockpit of the Navy's Most Lethal Aircraft, the F/A-18 Superhornet.* New York, NY: St. Martin's, 2019.

Craig Jones, *Fighting with Pride: LGBTQ in the Armed Forces.* Philadelphia, PA: Pen and Sword, 2019.

James McCartney, with Molly Sinclair McCartney, *America's War Machine: Vested Interests, Endless Conflicts.* New York, NY: Thomas Dunne, 2015.

David E. Rohall, Morton G. Ender, et al. (eds), *Inclusion in the American Military: A Force for Diversity.* Lanham, MD: Lexington, 2019.

Amy J. Rutenberg, *Rough Draft: Cold War Military Manpower Policy and the Origins of the Vietnam-Era Draft Resistance.* Ithaca, NY: Cornell University Press, 2019.

William A. Taylor, *Military Service and American Democracy from World War II to the Iraq and Afghanistan Wars.* Lawrence, KS: University Press of Kansas, 2019.

Pamela D. Toler, *Women Warriors: An Unexpected History.* Boston, MA: Beacon, 2019.

Lynn Vincent and Sara Vladic, *Indianapolis: The True Story of the Worst Sea Disaster in US Naval History and the 50-Year Fight to Exonerate an Innocent Man.* New York, NY: Simon and Schuster, 2018.

Jake Wood, *Once a Warrior: How One Veteran Found a New Mission Closer to Home.* New York, NY: Sentinel, 2020.

Index